A Love For Tomorrow

OYINKANSOLA OGUNYINKA

A Love For Tomorrow

Copyright © 2021 by Oyinkansola A. Ogunyinka

All rights reserved. No part of this book may be reproduced in any form without permission in writing from the publisher, except in the case of brief quotations embodied in critical articles or reviews.

DISCLAIMER

This novel is a work of fiction. Characters and events are the product of the author's imagination. Any resemblance to any person, living or dead, is coincidental.

All bible passages quoted from Common English Bible (CEB)

Editor: Omolara Ogunyinka

Cover Design: Basola Michael | AFRO Designs

What people are saying about ...

A Love for Tomorrow

I had goosebumps reading Oyinkan's book - the good kind of goosebumps you get when a piece of work makes you all warm and fuzzy, and connects with you in all the right places. It's creative, insightful and such an incredible read.

- Laju Iren,

Book Writing Coach, Filmmaker, Founder of the *Christian Story-teller Prize* and Best-selling Author of *Dating Intelligently*, the critically acclaimed *Selfies with Bible Girls*, *Loving Amanda* and *Finding Mariam.*

A Love for Tomorrow creates a world where love is not like the "books or movies". It's real; you're able to catch it, you're able to feel it.

- Stephanie Chizoba Odili,
Award-winning author of *Deafening Silence*

OYINKANSOLA OGUNYINKA

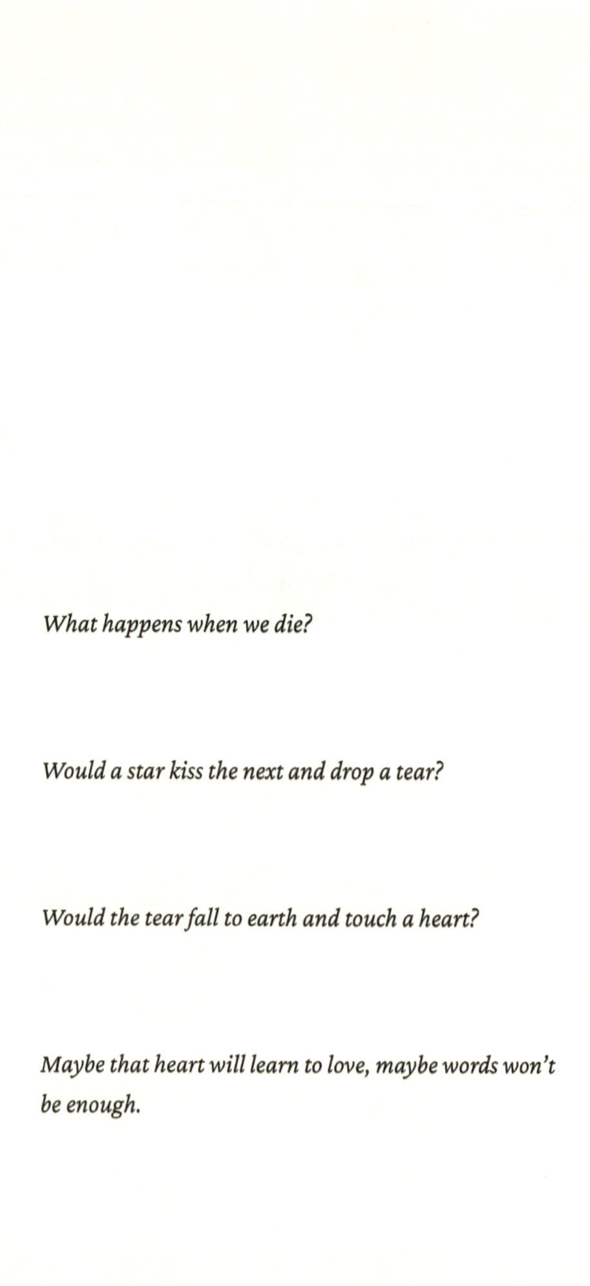

What happens when we die?

Would a star kiss the next and drop a tear?

Would the tear fall to earth and touch a heart?

Maybe that heart will learn to love, maybe words won't be enough.

The ones who love us will miss us.

As the sand beneath our feet covers graves we'll never know

Only memories keep alive the souls of those we've lost.

Contents

Prologue   XI

1. Chapter 1   1

2. Chapter 2   10

3. Chapter 3   20

4. Chapter 4   27

5. Chapter 5   35

6. Chapter 6   41

7. Chapter 7   47

8. Chapter 8   60

9. Chapter 9   69

10. Chapter 10   76

11. Chapter 11   85

12. Chapter 12   94

13. Chapter 13   104

14. Chapter 14   117

15. Chapter 15   125

16. Epilogue   131

Author's Note   134

Acknowledgments   136

About The Author   137

Prologue

California, USA | April 2019 |

'I can't do this anymore, Lord. Help me.' He muttered under his breath. Running both hands across his face, he let out a low groan. Frank had never been a man to act on impulse. He was very proper; organized, goal-driven and composed.

That was until he lost his wife in a brutal plane crash. Now...well now, he was a broken man. A very very broken man.

He watched his daughter Nora as she played around in her little bride's dress and the ghost of a smile played on his lips. She looked like a little angel and the sight took his breath away.

It broke his heart that Laura wasn't here to see her, and she wouldn't be here for every major milestone in their daughter's life either. The fact that she had died with their son still in her made him all the more depressed. You would think losing the love of your life so violently was enough pain for one to endure in a lifetime, but when she was also carrying your second child -your unborn son- well, pain seemed too mild a word to describe how he felt.

A sob caught in his throat as his eyes once again landed on the couple on the other side of the reception hall. The stars of the day, Taiwo and Karen, looked so happy and he was torn between sharing in their joy and wallowing in his own sorrow.

He missed her, so much that it hurt. Even after more than two years, he still closed his eyes sometimes and imagined her soft hands trailing his beards and then his lips before she dropped a kiss that made him lose all reason.

He imagined her bustling around in their house back home in Nigeria, fussing over him eating healthier and bossing Nora around. Laura, his sweet Laura, was gone and as usual, the thought made him weak in the knees.

Swallowing hard, he did a quick turn and walked pointedly towards the minibar and farther away from the dancing area.

Mixing a fairly strong cup of vodka and soda, he grabbed a window seat and took a sip. He was oblivious to the noise around him as he reminisced about the good old days with his wife and momentarily forgot that he was supposed to be watching Nora.

A loud shriek from behind him caught his attention and he looked back to somewhat of a scene in a corner of the hall. People were gathered around someone or something that seemed to fascinate them and the noise was obviously from there. He hurried over and weaved his way through the crowd to find out what the problem was. They all seemed to be murmuring about something.

'Get back you little brat!' It was the same voice he'd heard shrieking and it shocked him that it was coming from the beautiful lady he had seen walk in earlier with her little son. She held the boy close to her feet now and all her anger was directed at...Nora.

Nora's lower lips were trembling and she held her tiny bouquet of flowers so tightly he thought she'd squeeze it to nothingness.

'What's the problem?' He asked loud enough for everyone to turn towards him and stare. Nora ran to him the instant her eyes found his and she hid her face in his shirt when he scooped her into his arms. She was trembling so badly it almost brought tears to his eyes.

'The problem is...your little brat there was harassing my son!' She shouted again and gasps filled the air at the way she referred to Nora. She was obviously drunk.

'I'd appreciate it if you didn't use such words on my daughter. And she's only a child for heaven's sake. What could she have possibly said to...'

'Don't tell me what or what not to say man. Oh...I see what's going on here, you're trying to...' The rest of the words trailed off as a hiccup shook her off balance. Two more hiccups and she had thrown up all over the floor.

Gasps once again filled the air and the crowd shuffled backwards, keeping their distance.

It seemed someone had alerted the woman's family though because he saw a man who introduced himself as Tosan and an older lady hurry towards her and shuffle her away with her son. The older woman looked faintly familiar and he knew he must have met her once or twice before. As they passed in front of him, the man turned to Frank for a second and mumbled an apology.

'Shit.' He cussed under his breath and immediately regretted it. Nora was right there and she jerked her head up to look at him with big, innocent eyes.

'Daddy.'

'Yes honey.'

'Language.' Her little eyes seemed to chastise him and she pouted her lips disapprovingly even as he struggled to keep his cool.

'Sorry baby. I didn't mean to say that.'

'Hm.' She murmured, put her head back on his chest and wrapped her tiny arms around his neck. He clenched his teeth in barely contained anger and pushed through the crowd, ignoring their probing stares and side comments.

All he wanted was to get his baby out of there. And fast. This was no setting for a child. If anything, he was glad the ruckus hadn't drawn Taiwo or Karen's attention from the far side of the room. They'd find out later anyway.

'I didn't do it daddy. I was jus' dancing and then I hit him. But...it was a mistake. And then his drink spill'd. And and...he started to cry...and then...' her bottom lip quivered and she burst into tears then.

'I know baby. It's not your fault.' He patted her back and rocked back and forth as he made his way to their car.

'I wasn't trying t-t-to hurt an-a-anybody daddy. I promise.' She cried some more and he held her tighter, placing a kiss on her forehead.

'I know baby. I know. I got you now. I'm sorry I left you alone. I'm so so sorry.' He swallowed the lump in his own throat and sat with her in the back till she fell asleep on him, sucking her thumb.

Everything in him wanted to go back in there and cause a scene of his own, questioning them all, why they had let that crazy woman pick on his daughter, why no one had stopped her and more importantly, why the woman had gotten so drunk at a wedding.

Even as the thought occurred to him, he mentally chided himself. Hadn't he also been well on his way to getting drunk before the whole drama ensued? It really made him think. He'd been saying he'd stop drinking for ages now and this felt like the final straw. It could have been him in that lady's position. Alcohol did that to a person and he was done being a slave to it.

He wondered about the strange sadness that he'd seen in her eyes since the moment she walked in. He had felt pain, he still struggled with it and he knew a wounded soul when he saw one. This one needed healing, probably as much as he did. Or maybe even more.

Shaking off the dreary feeling around him, he dropped Nora in the back seat and prepared for the ride back to the hotel. He thought of how lonely it would be, going back to his apartment in Canada after the wedding. Yes, he had initially relocated there from Nigeria to help him heal and it had helped- in a way- but now, he just felt restless and dissatisfied.

Now that he thought about it again, he didn't really feel like returning to Canada. The apartment always felt so cold and empty and he hadn't done much to grow his business since he moved over two years ago.

Bringing himself to do it had not been easy but he flew from Canada to America just to attend Taiwo's wedding. And he knew it wasn't only because he was Laura's brother. No. Taiwo had been through a lot himself yet he had always been a constant pillar of support for Frank through his pain. Taiwo was like a brother to him.

He sometimes felt guilty that he was depriving Nora of growing up around family and living a normal life and in all honesty, he missed home too.

Then go back. The still small voice in his head whispered.

'Don't fear, because I am with you; don't be afraid, for I am your God. I will strengthen you, I will surely help you; I will hold you with my righteous strong hand.'

Isaiah 41:10 played in his head and he felt himself relax.

He knew it was God leading him because he felt at peace with the thought. Like a bright light shone on his path, his next move became very clear and simple to him; he was going back home to Nigeria. And something told him that this time, things would be better. It felt right and he was completely peaceful about the decision. All he could do now was hope and pray.

To any random onlooker, he had become quite impulsive and in truth, maybe he had. Grief had weird effects on people and his move to Canada had been quite impulsive. But moving back to Nigeria? This was God. And he felt it in the very fiber of his being. Impulsive or not.

Chapter 1

Frank walked into the bookstore with a deep frown etched on his face. He was just coming from dropping his daughter off at her dance rehearsals and to say the Lagos traffic hadn't dealt with him would be the greatest lie of the century.

He had considered cancelling her class for the day but he knew Nora, she would never let him hear the end of it. She was a tiny, adorable 7-year old terrorist. As he walked towards the counter, he was grateful for the cool gust of breeze that hit him from the air conditioner in the corner of the room.

'Hello' he muttered to the lady at the counter whose head was buried in a book.

'Uh!' She jumped with a start and looked up in embarrassment, rushing to adjust her glasses and smoothen her hair.

The first thing that hit him when she looked up were her eyes. They looked vaguely familiar and…

'You said?' She interrupted his train of thought.

'I-I said...hello.'

'Hello sir. How may I help you please?' She watched him through her red rimmed glasses wondering why he was still standing there instead of getting what he needed. 'Looking for any book in particular?' She asked again.

'Um, no.' He stood up straighter, slightly embarrassed that she had caught him staring. 'I am actually here to see Christian. I called him already.'

'Christian?' She looked confused and for a split second, Frank wondered if he was in the right place. Had two years away faded his memory? He didn't think so.

'Yes, Christian. Christian Olumuyiwa.'

'Ooooh, you mean Mr. Olumuyiwa?' She facepalmed and looked up sheepishly. 'I'm sorry. He's my boss so I don't really call him that. I forget it's his name sometimes. You know how these things are. You know it one second, the next minute it's gone. You know what I mean?'

'Right.' He nodded, an amused smile playing on his lips.

'I'm blabbing.' She bit her lips and ran her hand through her braids. 'Sorry sir. Um, he actually stepped out for lunch, he should be back any moment now. Please, take a seat.'

'Thank you.' He flashed her a smile and sat down on a cozy sofa in the small make-shift reception. Most of the store's space was taken up by bookshelves and quirky art pieces. Running his eyes across the room briefly, he struggled to find a blank spot on the walls. Just like Christian to cover every available wall space with art.

The store looked the same as he remembered it from three years ago; except that the shelves had a fresh coat of paint and of course, Christian had apparently hired a new attendant. All well and good, the other lady had been a bit too cold anyway and not nearly as beautiful as this one. Speaking of beautiful, she was walking towards him right now and for some reason, his palms got a little sweaty.

'Would you like anything to drink? Water, ice tea, juice?' She asked him casually.

'Water would be great right now.'

'Alright then. I'll be right back. And so should Mr. Olumuyiwa.' She left him and disappeared into a back room. Just as she walked back in with a cold bottle of water, the door opened and Christian walked in.

'Speak of the...' A smile split Frank's face and he stood up to meet him.

'Don't say devil.' Christian said cheekily and they both burst out laughing before hugging each other. It was a brief man-hug with shoulder patting and a handshake after. Typical.

'How have you been, man?'

'Good, good. We're pushing.' They hugged again.

'So, you didn't want to come and visit me right? Haven't you been back for months?' Christian accused him playfully.

'Mehn, I've been trying to settle down *egbon*. This Lagos traffic and heat is a problem on it's own. *E ma binu.*'

Christian laughed and nudged him. 'Hm, shut up there. Because you travelled for a minute now we won't hear word again. Where's Nora *jare*?'

'I just dropped her off at dance practice. I'll visit with her one of these days, don't worry.'

Christian nodded and turned towards the attendant. She had been standing there awkwardly with a bottle of water in her hands throughout the whole exchange. He gave Christian a pointed look that said introduce-me-already and he got the hint.

'Seun, I see you've met my brother. But, let me do the proper introductions.'

She almost balked at the word brother. At that point she wanted to enter the ground. She had made her boss' brother wait in the reception. Why on earth didn't he mention it? And why did they suddenly look so alike? She hadn't noticed that before.

'Frank, this is Seun, my PA and store attendant. Seun, this is Frank, my only sibling in the whole world.' Christian continued, placing emphasis on the 'whole'.

'You're so dramatic bro.' Frank shook his head and flashed Seun a smile. They looked alike for sure but Frank was obviously younger and way more handsome.

'Hi Seun, nice to meet you.'

'Nice to meet you too sir. I've heard a lot about you.' She smiled back and stretched her hand out for a shake. Frank ignored it and moved in for a light kiss on her cheeks.

She blinked and stole a glance at Christian. He had a funny look on his face. Maybe he found it inappropriate, it was sort of unexpected.

'All good things I hope?' Frank asked, not really expecting an answer. She smiled and nodded. 'Let's talk later okay.' He winked over his shoulder at her and followed Christian into his office.

'Frank.' Christian turned to him the moment the door was closed and they had both sat down.

'Yes.'

'Frank.'

'What na?' He looked up from his phone at his brother and scrunched his nose.

'What was that all about?'

'What was what all about?' He feigned ignorance.

'Oh don't play dumb with me. We're too old for that.'

'I don't know what you're talking about.' The ghost of a smile played on his lips and he unconsciously scratched his beards.

'What with the kissing and flirting? And I saw you looking at her before I walked in. Have anything to share little bro?'

'Don't call me little, you know I hate that. And kissing? Really Christian? I think you're exaggerating. It was more of…a light peck. And I was just being friendly.' Frank defended himself and rolled his eyes.

'Friendly?'

'Yes. Friendly.' He put his phone down and picked up a book that caught his attention: Tomorrow is Another Day. The title was intriguing and he made a mental note to borrow it before he left.

'Okay bro. Whatever you say.' Christian held his hands up and reclined in his chair. 'Now are we going to catch up or what?'

Frank rolled his eyes again and shot his brother a sheepish smile. 'Sure, let's do that.'

***

Unlike when he had come in, there were now 3 ladies at the counter, chattering on about God-knows-what and giggling like school girls as Seun packaged their purchases. Frank was happy for the quiet when they left. He didn't exactly know why but he walked towards the counter and leaned on it, pretending to be checking out a bracelet on display.

'How much is this?' He blurted.

She looked up at him for the second time that day and then shifted her gaze to the bracelet. For the split second her eyes caught his, a flash of recognition crossed his mind but he just couldn't place it. He felt like he had met her before.

'It's 2000 naira sir.' She raised an eyebrow and turned to her computer. The price was written on the bracelet, why was he asking her and staring like a weirdo?

'Are you getting it?' She asked.

'Yes yes.' He passed her his card and shook his head mentally. What was all this school boy nervousness? He hardly even noticed women in the past few years, talkless of flirting with them and getting fidgety. On the bright side, at least the bracelet wouldn't waste away in the house. He'd give it to Nora. Two thousand naira well spent. Who was he kidding? Nora was more of a necklace person. She still wore the one her mother gave her years ago, afraid to take it off and forget her.

'Thanks.' He mumbled and collected the nylon from her. After thinking of what to say to prolong their conversation to no avail, he shook his head. He was giving up when she looked at him again and spoke.

'Why didn't you tell me you were Mr. Olumuyiwa's brother?' Her eyes pierced into his and he blinked. The feeling that he had met her before came over him for the umpteenth time that day.

'Oh. That. I didn't think it was necessary. Would it have made any difference?'

'Would it have made any...' She shook her head, exasperated and looked at him with mild irritation. 'This is Nigeria Mr. Frank. It would have made all the difference. What if I had mistakenly said the wrong thing? My job would probably be on the line right now.'

'What makes you think you didn't?'

"*Ehn?*'

'Say the wrong thing I mean. What makes you think you didn't say the wrong thing?' He smirked and twirled the nylon around his fingers.

'W-what?' Her eyes grew larger and she squirmed in her seat.

'Relax. I'm messing with you.'

'Haha.' She laughed nervously and adjusted her glasses. This man was unnerving her and she didn't like it. All she wanted was to go back to reading her book.

'See you around.'

'Okay Mr. Frank.'

'Call me Frank. The Mr. makes me feel old.'

Okay...Frank.' He winked and waved lightly before walking out.

Her eyes trailed him as he left and she breathed a long sigh of relief as the door closed behind him. She couldn't explain it but his presence had made her jumpy. She really couldn't tell why but somewhere in her mind, she wasn't sure she wanted to explore the thought.

The man was easy on the eyes, she'd give him that. And yeah, his kiss - well, peck - had felt good but it ended up making her feel embarrassed, leaving her hand hanging and her boss gawking.

It'd probably be best if she banished thoughts about Frank from her mind completely. The man might even be married. Hadn't Mr Olumuyiwa mentioned a daughter? But if he was married, why hadn't he asked about a wife? Did he wear a wedding ring? She couldn't quite remember. Baby mama maybe?

Before she could make any further assumptions, he walked back in, nodded at her briefly and rushed into Mr Olumuyiwa's office. While she was still trying to process the whole thing, he had rushed back out, book in hand.

He caught her looking at him and raised his hands to show the book well. 'I forgot something.' He said and shrugged. When he raised his hands, she noted, as hard as she tried not to, that he wore no ring. Okay, so maybe she hadn't tried hard enough.

She squinted to see the book's title through her glasses: Tomorrow is Another Day.

That was her book, the one she wrote. No one knew though; just her mother and her publishers. She loved the freedom and power that writing anonymously gave her, some people judged her awfully, but no one could do it to her face because they didn't know her.

'Got it.' She gave him a thumbs up before he hurried out again. Now that was weird. It occurred to her that she wasn't very comfortable with him reading her life story but then again, he didn't know her. And even if he did eventually find out that it was her story, hadn't she written and published it herself? The plan was obviously to have people read it.

And he's not going to find out.

She shook off the thought and got back to reading her book. She would be off in a few hours and her son's nanny would go home. She needed to cash in on all the reading time she could get before her time would be swallowed up by Uzi for the rest of the day.

Besides, she had bigger problems on her mind.

Like Dozie.

She banished the thought and continued reading. She didn't want to think about her son's father right now. Or ever again. He reminded her of all her life's mistakes.

***

Just as Frank got into his car, it finally dawned on him where he had met her before. That mildly irritated look on her face when he asked if telling her he was Christian's brother would have made any difference was all it took for the memories to come flying through the windows of his mind. He almost chuckled at the thought; she had been so defensive.

They met at Taiwo's wedding party months ago. She was piss drunk at the time while he was only slightly buzzed and she had made a scene for something very insignificant. She had that same irritated look on her face but it had been even worse that day. And of course, she hadn't been wearing what he assumed were her reading glasses.

It was all coming back to him now. No wonder he hadn't remembered her immediately, booze was in play. Otherwise, he was super good with faces.

He wondered a little at the fact that she didn't recognize him in any way. Though, he somewhat loved the mystery around it all. Seun had intrigued him from that very first encounter and now that they met again, his interest only grew.

He might not have had the courage to ask for her number today but he'd surely get it, even if it meant bullying Christian for it.

Chapter 2

Apapa, Lagos, Nigeria | June 2019 |

Seun drove into the familiar premises and a small smile played on her lips as Uzi jumped up and down in the back seat.

'Going to see Grandma!' He giggled and repeated the words, pulling at her seatbelt. He was so excited and she couldn't blame him; she was just as excited, maybe even more. Since she made the decision to move out after publishing her book, she had considered coming back so many times.

Temi's Home was safe, everyone and everything was familiar and most importantly, Temi was always there for her.

Sometimes in the past few months, she felt she had made a mistake moving out and maybe she had. Temi had tried to talk her out of it but she wouldn't let up because she convinced herself it was the best decision at the time.

The move had given her time to think and learn a thing or two about independence but it had also brought Dozie crashing back into her life and breaking down her fragile defenses like an arrangement of dominoes.

Even though he was Uzi's father, Dozie was bad news and she knew him enough to know that he wouldn't give up trying to get to her now that he had found her again. So here she was, moving back in with her mum and hoping to get some semblance of normalcy again.

She passed by the playground and a wave of nostalgia washed over her. Parking right beside Temi's old Toyota, she smiled a little and sank back into the car seat. The old woman refused to sell it or get another one and Seun couldn't understand it for the life of her.

She remembered the last time she had tried to talk Temi into getting a new car. She had only just had Uzi then and was fresh out of rehab.

'Mummy, you need to get rid of this piece of trash. It has seen better days.' Seun whined as they chugged along the road in the ancient car.

'Hm. Hm.' Temi shrugged and shook her head. 'It's as good as new.'

'No it's not. You need a new car mummy and we both know you can afford it. Aah ah. Good as new ke?'

'What do you know?' She laughed and shot Seun a look. 'This car is older than you o. I don't need a new car baby.'

Seun threw her hands up in surrender as she sighed, exasperated. 'I give up.'

'Mummy.' Uzi's voice dragged her back to reality. The memory faded away and she was once again, back in her car, sitting in front of her mother's house, gathering the courage to go in.

Taking a deep breath, she stepped out of the car feeling stupid all over again. She should have called Temi to let her know she was coming but she was too chicken to do it and now she was here.

Unannounced.

What if she didn't take her in? What would she do then?

What if she takes you in though? Her subconscious voice nudged her. Muttering a quick prayer, she walked with Uzi to the front door. This was it. It was now or never.

'Mummy, are you okay?' Uzi asked her, placing a hand on her right lap and looking up at her. 'No I'm not okay!' she wanted to scream. Instead, she swallowed back tears and rubbed his head lovingly.

'Mummy is fine baby. Mummy's fine.'

She clenched and unclenched her free hand, mentally slapping herself for not having the guts to call. She knocked before she could talk herself out of it and the door opened almost immediately. She blinked once, twice and then stared.

'H-hi...' Frank muttered, a look of instant recognition came on his face.

She suddenly felt small and inadequate under his soft gaze. She squirmed and for a split second, she considered turning back, getting into her car and going back to beg her landlord to give her her apartment back. But she hadn't come this far to give up without trying so she braced herself and spoke.

'Hi.' Her voice came out stronger than she felt and she was grateful.

'Seun right?' He flashed her a smile. She nodded and looked everywhere but at him.

'What are you doing here?' They both spoke at the same time and stopped.

Talk about awkwardness.

'Sorry...'

'Uh, I mean...'

They spoke together again and Seun bit her lip. *Really?*

'You go. Ladies first.' Frank urged her.

She considered making a big deal about his act of chivalry but then thought better against it. What would she even say? There was no use making the man an enemy and she didn't even have the energy.

'I actually came to see Temi.' It was a half-truth but there was no way she was baring her soul to this stranger. He might be reading her book but he didn't know her and he was her boss' brother and Temi's whatever-she-was-to-him. The last thing she wanted was to share her past and end up looking stupid in front of him.

'Yeah me too. I'm a new volunteer so I'm getting 'oriented'.' Frank smiled again and her heart started to beat faster. Her nerves were already on edge as it was and now he was making her more self conscious.

What is wrong with you Seun? So what if the man is volunteering here and you're moving back in? He's not the first man in the world and he won't be the last. Focus woman!

She shook her head and smiled back. 'That's nice.'

It was only a matter of time before he found out why she was really here. So much for the half truth.

'And who do we have here?' Frank turned his attention to Uzi who was getting restless beside his mother. He knew this was her son but he still asked. The woman didn't recognize him anyway and it wouldn't hurt to know the boy's name. The only resemblance between mother and son was their piercing eyes and he concluded that the boy must look very much like his father.

'Oh, this is my son Uzi.' She smiled in spite of herself and stroked Uzi's head; he always made her happy. 'Uzi, greet uncle.'

'Good afternoon uncle.' Uzi muttered, oblivious to the tension between his mother and 'uncle'.

Seun wasn't sure how long they had been standing there and even though she was initially worried about Temi's reaction, she breathed a sigh of relief when the older woman appeared in the doorway.

'Seun.' Temi's eyes widened and she stared in shock for a few seconds before rushing forward to enclose her in a hug.

Seun closed her eyes and melted into the hug, basking in all the warmth. A lone tear rolled down her eye and she didn't bother with wiping it off. 'Grandma!' Uzi joined the hug and she pulled him closer. How had she ever thought that Temi would turn them away? This woman loved her and her son like her own.

***

Frank looked on in mild surprise as they hugged each other like long lost lovers. It was as though they didn't even remember that he was there. Whatever was happening, it was beautiful and he continued observing them in silence. He would find out soon enough.

'Frank, this is Seun, my daughter and her son, my grandson, Uzi. Seun, Frank.' Temi pulled out of the hug and smiled, never taking her eyes off Seun.

If only she knows that we've met, Frank thought to himself. He looked at Seun with a knowing smile and stretched out his hands for a handshake. She took it.

'Nice to meet you Frank.' Seun spoke, looking behind his head. She couldn't look him in the eye and he raised an eyebrow.

'The feeling is mutual.' They were both putting up a charade and it amused him to no end.

'Let's go in shall we?' Temi herded them in and closed the door, oblivious to the growing tension.

As they settled in, Frank didn't miss the confused look that crossed Nora's eyes when they landed on Seun and Uzi. *Oh boy.*

'My daughter, Nora.' He introduced her.

'Good afternoon ma.' Nora greeted Seun before turning accusing eyes to him. The look on his face was the don't-look-at-me-I-didn't-plan-this look. She scrunched her nose and turned back to her puzzle book. *Just great.*

They sat in awkward silence as Temi stepped out to get more drinks and snacks and Frank wished he could say or do something to address the elephant in the room. He noted the hostility between the children and groaned inwardly. They obviously remembered the wedding incident.

He almost felt sorry about Seun's bewilderment when she told Uzi to 'go play puzzle' with Nora and she quickly replied with a vehement 'No!' She still didn't remember them.

Thankfully, Temi got back soon enough and Seun excused herself and Uzi into the kitchen so they could finish their talk. She let Uzi go to the playground while she spent the whole time practicing her speech to Temi. She still wasn't sure of how Temu would react anyway. Her welcome had been warm no doubt but moving back in was a whole different ball game.

When Frank left, Seun hurried to the living room. Temi looked at her pensively, waiting for her to speak. She hadn't seen her in months and she wanted to hear her out. This daughter of hers was a hard nut to crack; always had been. But beneath her facade of strength, she was just a child hungry for love and acceptance.

Seun wanted to rush everything out before she lost her nerve but as she knelt before her mother and opened her mouth to speak, words failed her.

'Ahn ah, why? Don't kneel now. Come sit beside me.' Temi held her hands and tried to pull her up. She refused and buried her face in Temi's laps.

'Mummy…' The words caught in her throat as sobs racked through her body.

'Oh Seun, stop it. Why? Ahn ah.'

'Mummy, I'm sorry. I was so stupid. I'm sorry…'

'Don't worry baby. I'm not angry at you. Stand up.'

'But you should be.' She kept crying. 'I left you after everything you warned me about.'

'You're here now aren't you? Forget about it. It's in the past.' Temi comforted her.

'I thought I could do it on my own but I was wrong. You were right, I'm not ready. I've made a mess of things.'

Temi kept patting her back soothingly, like a baby; her baby. 'It's alright baby. Oya stand up and sit down.' She tapped the space beside her and waited for Seun to sit. 'Don't beat yourself up about it. What's done is done, hm?'

'Yes ma.'

'So all I want to know now is what you want. What do you want?'

Seun almost broke into tears again at how much love she was showing her after everything. 'I want peace mummy. A-and…' She stuttered for a second before continuing. 'I want to move back in.'

Temi turned to look at her. 'Are you sure?' She was happy for sure, she had been waiting for this day for months. But she wanted to be sure that Seun felt good about this. Seun was only twenty three and she was still a child in so many ways; she didn't need to be living alone. Especially not with everything she had been through in this life. Still, she sensed that there was something else Seun was not telling her.

'I'm sure mummy. If you'll have me that is...' She sounded un-sure.

'Of course, I'll have you. I love you Seun. And I love Uzi too. I'll never turn you guys away.' Temi pulled her in for a side hug swallowing the lump in her throat.

'Ah thank God. If you said no, I don't know what I'd have done. All our things are in the car mummy. Like, maybe we'd have had to sleep in the car and I'd go and beg oga landlord tomorrow.' They both burst out laughing.

'Still as cheeky as ever aren't you?' Temi pinched her playfully.

'You know you love me.' Seun stuck her tongue out and rolled her eyes.

'Yes I do. I love you very much.' Temi closed her eyes and inhaled deeply, praying even as she asked that it wasn't what she feared. 'You're not telling me something Seun. What is it?'

Seun sat up straight and squirmed, weighing her options in her head. She could either lie or tell the truth. She concluded that there was no point lying to her mother; she knew everything about her anyway. 'H-h-he came back.' She mumbled.

Oh God, please no. 'Who?' Temi wanted to be sure.

'Dozie.' Seun replied flatly.

'Seun!' Temi's tone was reprimanding and Seun shrank back. She hated it when Temi scolded her.

'Mummy, you have to believe me. I don't know how he found us. I don't.' Seun whispered.

'Hm...' Temi looked lost in thought for a few seconds. 'But you're sleeping with him again abi.' It was more of a statement than a question.

Seun wanted to run and hide. She knew her mother; she would dig out dirt till she found the buried bone. 'No.'

'Don't lie to me Seun.'

'I'm not ly...' Temi shot her a warning look and she faltered. She let out a low breath and sighed. 'It was just once.'

'That's it. We're getting a restraining order Seun.'

'Mummy!'

'Don't mummy me!' She snapped at her.

'There's no need for you to do that.' Seun's right hand massaged her forehead slowly as she held back tears. 'Besides mummy, nobody says restraining order in Nigeria.' She muttered under her breath.

'There is every need, Seun. And that's not the point. Restraining order, court injunction, same thing. That guy is trouble and he has proved it well enough. You talked me into not pressing charges after the idiot abused you physically and emotionally. Don't even get me started on the drugs. The man tried to make you abort Uzi Seun!' Temi was livid now.

'He's better now.' Her voice was little more than a squeal now.

'No, he is not. And you know it. I am tired of having these conversations Seun. That boy shouldn't ever be anywhere around you or Uzi. We are getting a restraining order.' She paused for a second, as if deciding between sticking to the Netflix friendly 'restraining order' or using more local vocabulary. She settled on the latter. 'Or court injunction. Whatever it's called, we are getting it!'

'Okay.' Silent tears rolled down her eyes and Temi pulled her into a hug.

'It's for your own safety baby. And Uzi's too. You know I'm right.'

'Yes mummy. I know.'

Later that night, Seun lay in bed and cried into her pillow. She couldn't understand why she protected the idiot so much. He had ruined her life so terribly and she would still be wallowing in those ruins by now if not for Temi. Why on earth did she fall back into his arms when he showed up again?

God help me, she prayed. She wasn't the best of Christians but Temi believed in God and He made her happy. She wanted to be happy so bad.⬤

Chapter 3

Surulere, Lagos, Nigeria | July 2019 |

Frank rolled around in his bed and struggled to find sleep. It had been two weeks since he ran into Seun again at Temi's Home. He saw her a few times after he started volunteering but he mainly stayed clear of the main house and focused on teaching IT skills to the children.

She seemed like she needed her space and he didn't exactly understand why he was so attracted to her in the first place. She was very beautiful but she was also way younger than him. Besides, he was still healing and she obviously had her own baggage.

Yet, he found himself drawn to her all the time. It didn't make any sense.

'Urgh!' He muttered to the empty room. 'Get out of my head! I don't need this right now.'

Maybe you do. Ah, the famous still quiet voice in his head.

'But Lord...' He protested and listened for the voice again. Nothing came.

He released the breath he had been holding and scratched his beard. He didn't want to think about it anymore.

Taking a shower, he checked in on Nora in her room and smiled. His ray of sunshine. Their conversation when they left Temi's home that evening stayed glued to his memory.

'Daddy, I don't like them.'

'Who?' He feigned ignorance

'That aunty and her child.'

'Nora, you shouldn't say things like that.' He grimaced and asked God for help on how to handle the situation.

'Why? She was very mean to me that time that we went to Uncle Taiwo's wedding.'

'Yes, but she's sorry. You have to forgive and forget.' He tried again.

'She didn't say sorry. How do you know she's really sorry? Why do I have to forgive her?'

'I know baby, but I'm sure she feels sorry. And you should forgive her, because you're a good girl.'

Nora pouted and looked out the window in defiance. The simple act reminded him of Laura and he swallowed hard.

'She's not a good aunty.'

'Ah ahn Nora. You know Jesus would want you to forgive her. We are called to love remember?'

'Yes.' She said after a few seconds.

'Good. So you promise to start liking her?'

She smiled at him dryly. 'I'll try.'

'But you like Grandma Temi right?'

'I guess so.' She shrugged and tried to sound uninterested. But he saw the ghost of a smile play on her lips. She liked Grandma Temi a lot and he was sure the snacks and puzzle book she gave her were largely responsible for that. Thank God for small miracles.

'Alright baby.' He sighed. *He knew that was the best he'd get out of her and he decided to let it rest for now. She'd come around soon; or at least he hoped so.*

He closed Nora's door quietly and went back to his room. Turning on his side, his eye caught the book he borrowed from Christian a little over a month ago. It had been on his bedside drawer since that day and he finally decided to open it. He might as well. He couldn't sleep anyway and he didn't want his mind drifting towards thoughts of the company he'd sold to move back to Nigeria and start afresh. So, he started reading...

***

Entry One - June, 2018

All I want is to live a normal life, like the other kids. I don't have too many wishes or wants and I've learned that keeping to myself helps me avoid a lot of trouble. Whenever the shouting starts, I just hole up in my room and try to block out the sounds.

And if it gets worse, physical maybe, I move to the bathroom and run a cold bath.

I usually turn on the shower and lay naked in the tub, letting the sound of the water drown out their noises, allowing the cool water soothe my nerves, pretending to be anywhere else but here.

The shouts never really go away though, because for one, I have heard them argue so many times. I know the pattern. And two, they are just always too loud.

You know I always wonder why the neighbors never do anything. I know they hear. They hear. The whole street hears them. Why does no one ever do or say anything?

My silent tears would mix with the water running down my body and I would bite down the urge to scream, scream at them to stop. I remember trying that once. God, it was terrible. The yelling turned on me and for the first time, I realized; I am the problem.

At least that's what I think.

***

Entry Two - July, 2018

Mummy always says she stayed because of me and I believe her. I was only nine when she first told me and though I am older now, it has been my truth for such a long time.

I know that she is just terrified of leaving but I still can't stop believing I am not at least a part of the problem.

Mummy is terrified of being alone. She can't be alone, she doesn't know how to be. And so she stays. And suffers.

Dad suffers too and so do I. We all do.

I am not even sure when the fights and beatings first started but they get worse every time.

Some days I consider killing myself, so that it will just end. But I am a coward. I really am.

I can't do it.

***

'Wow'. Frank thought before closing the book. The intensity of the writer's emotions flooded through him as he read each word and he found himself curious about him/her. He turned to the front page and checked the writer's name; Tabitha was all it said; no last name. At least now he knew the writer was a 'her'. Turning the back cover, he got even more puzzled.

I am not your typical writer. I can not claim to be a master of this art. But I write my heart in words and hope that you will feel it beat. This is a true story and I published it because I am a little crazy. Also, my editor said it was 'moving'. Don't feel sorry for me when you read this and please, don't stop reading when it gets too painful because it will. Just be a little kinder, show a little more humility and love a little more. I am Tabitha and I have learnt that being perfectly imperfect is nothing to be ashamed of. Read more of my works at tabithatheanon.com

'A true story hm...' He scratched his beard and lay on his back, staring at his ceiling intensely. His heart went out to this Tabitha woman and he wished he could find her and give her a long hug. He wanted to tell her that she didn't deserve all that she'd been through. She had only been a child. Closing his eyes in anguish, he placed a hand over his heart and muttered a prayer: *Lord please help her.*

At that moment, all thoughts of his own pain had vanished, he felt like he was reliving the woman's pain. With his eyes still closed, the scenes from the book played around in his mind. He didn't miss a beat as he reached for his phone and turned on his mobile data. Ignoring all the notifications that poured in, he navigated to the browser and typed her site url. What he saw almost broke him.

Ever heard of sublimation? Well, that's what this is for me. My therapist says channeling my negative emotions into creativity would help me handle them better. So I started writing. Don't worry, they're not all sad. No need to feel too much pity. Haha! Start reading at your own risk though.

He read from blog post to blog post; poems on domestic abuse, unrequited love, self-hate; stories of social misfits, weird medical conditions and death. The posts were a lot and he read as if hypnotized. Tabithatheanon had thousands of followers and he saw comments mirroring his thoughts.

'Who is Tabitha the anon? Show us your face.'

'These are amazing T. How do you do it?'

'I'm also in therapy Tabitha. I channel my own impulses into painting. Thanks for sharing with us.'

'Like this comment if you're here because you read the book!'

'Tell us your real name we want to know you.'

'Where have you been all my life?'

There were hundreds of comments and she replied most of them. There were also bad comments, ranging from thinly disguised sarcasm to full blown trolling. She didn't reply to those though but she didn't delete them either. This Tabitha was an enigma. He also found blog posts that had been removed because they were 'episodes' of what was now her book.

'I have to keep reading…even though it hurts. It's what she wanted.' He thought to himself and picked the book again. Just as he flipped the page to start chapter three, his alarm went off.

06:00am

He couldn't believe he had been reading for over four hours and hadn't noticed. Now it was time for work and he'd gotten no sleep. He waited for the feeling of annoyance to wash over him at all the factors in the universe that conspired to steal his rest but it didn't come. Instead, he felt calm; like he'd been doing the right thing.

Even though he had never met this Tabitha before, he felt like he knew her already. She wrote her unfiltered thoughts and why should she not? No one knew who she was anyway. What freedom!

He checked the time again and saw that fifteen minutes had passed. Throwing the book in his laptop bag, he woke Nora up and prepared her for school while he got ready for work. The schoolbus would be here in no time and he also needed to get to the orphanage and set up the computer lab. Whoever said volunteering was an easy task. He hoped he'd be able to keep reading during his break.□

Chapter 4

Yaba, Lagos, Nigeria | July 2019 |

Running under the rain in heels and a pencil skirt was not part of Seun's plan for the day. She normally wouldn't even wear heels or a skirt, talk less of a pencil skirt. But she had a meeting planned with her editor today and though the woman had literally made her career, her presence intimidated Seun to no end. She had so much charisma, everything about her life seemed perfect and not a strand of hair was ever out of place on her head. And oh yeah, she was a stickler for heels and a skirt, which explained the dressing; Seun wanted to please her today.

But as Tinubu's Lagos would have it, rain started falling as she made her way from the taxi to the entrance of the office complex. Typical. Not many things had been going her way for a while now so she shouldn't have been surprised, but she was. How on earth was no one else in the compound caught in this downpour with her? Why did the rain have to start just as the taxi dropped her off and drove away?

'Why me? Why today?' She whined and tried for the hundredth time to cover her hair with a newspaper as she lugged her heavy handbag along. Brushing a strand of hair from her eyes, she looked up and ran smack into someone. Everything in her hands flew in all directions and she muttered some obscenities before looking daggers in the person's direction.

'Don't you look where you're going? Imagine...' She adjusted her glasses and stopped dead in her tracks as she saw who it was. It was Frank, hunky Frank who was her boss' brother, the one who kept showing up everywhere she went and rattling her nerves, the one who made her skin tingle, the one she had been avoiding. Yup. It was him, in full flesh and blood. And, he had an umbrella. She stared at him for a split second before snapping back to reality when he spoke.

'I'm so sorry. I didn't mean to.' He rushed and bent down just as she did. 'Let me help you with those.' She bit back a snarky comment, pursed her lips in annoyance and let him help her. They huddled under his umbrella and hurried into the reception. The moment they got in, she turned to him.

'You can go now. I'm fine thank you.' She muttered, trying to collect her bag from him. She wanted to make herself as small as possible as people stared at her tactlessly. He insisted on waiting to make sure she was okay so she excused herself to try and salvage her wardrobe situation and makeup.

After spending almost fifteen minutes trying to make herself look presentable, she realised there was nothing she could do about the shirt. It was soaked through and had become indecently transparent and revealing.

She removed her glasses and cleaned them. Biting her lips, she stared at her reflection in the mirror. If Mrs. Dede tolerated her before, she was definitely going to judge her now. The woman

never really did or said anything untowards to her but she always just felt so inadequate around her, seeing as the woman knew her entire life, all the ugly, unspeakable details.

With a firm tilt of her chin, she decided that she wasn't going to see her editor anymore today. At least not looking like this. Grabbing some paper towels, she dabbed at her face again, scowling at her reflection in the mirror. She put the glasses back on.

Knock. Knock. Knock.

Who on earth could be knocking on the door of the ladies' restroom? Let her just enter na, Seun thought.

Knock. Knock. Knock.

'Urgh! Who is this clown?' She muttered and turned towards the door, facepalming.

'Hey Seun, are you okay in there?' It was Frank. *Oh Lord.*

'Uh, yes yes, I'm fine.'

'You've been in there for thirty minutes woman. If you're fine then come on out already.' He sounded frustrated and she almost felt sorry for him.

'I'll be out in a minute!' She looked at her reflection one last time before mustering the courage to go out. Folding her hands protectively across her chest, she stepped out, keeping her eyes to the ground.

'Ah you're alive. For a second there, I thought a monster had flushed you down the toilet.' He joked. She scrunched her face and smiled sheepishly, her hands still folded.

'Ha, funny.' Rolling her eyes, she cleared her throat and spoke again. 'I'm fine.'

He gave her a look that clearly said he didn't believe her. 'Of course, I can see that.' His tone dripped with sarcasm. 'Here, take my jacket.' He took off his denim jacket and handed it to her.

She didn't take it and she didn't say anything either. Instead, she shifted her gaze back to the ground and wondered how on earth she had gotten herself into this. From below her lashes, she took in how good he looked in his bodycon t-shirt and she swallowed hard. God took time creating this one, she thought.

And here she was, looking like a drowning rat. Humiliation washed over her again and she squared her shoulders, ready to tell him once more that she was fine and he could leave. She looked up at him and opened her mouth to talk but he held a hand up to stop her.

'Oh cut the crap Seun. I know, you're independent and can handle things on your own. You don't need a man to save you. I get it. But just admit it, you are not fine.' He studied her pensively and watched as her eyes darted everywhere but at him.

'You need some help right now and I don't see any other prince...or princess charmings hanging around these corridors offering to help you. So are you going to let me help you or what?'

She looked him in the eye this time, biting her lips. 'Okay.' She wished there was more she could say but Frank had hit closer to him than she cared to admit. Plus, she really just wanted to go home.

'Good.' He handed her the jacket and she took it this time, wrapping it around her body and biting down a shiver. She hated that he was right but the jacket felt so warm.

'So, what did you come to the Empire Towers to do?' He asked her. Ah, the question she had been dreading.

'Uh, I came to see a friend.'

'A friend? Oh great, me too. Do you want to go into her office? Or...' he let his words trail off.

'So eager to get rid of me already Prince Charming?' She baited him. He didn't bite.

'Nice try lady.'

'How do you know I didn't come to see a guy?' She tried again. A look she couldn't explain flashed across his face for a split second and it was almost like she had imagined it.

'Right. I'm sorry for assuming.'

'I'm kidding.' She nudged him playfully and laughed.

'Surprise surprise. The woman has a funny bone in her. Who would have thought?' He said it dryly and even though she knew he was joking, it hit a nerve.

'I'm not that bad Frank.' She sobered up and wrapped the jacket tighter around her. Her defenses were up again.

'Maybe not. But, I just haven't ever seen you laugh.'

'Maybe I don't have much to laugh about.' The words left her lips before she could think them through and now they were gone. She couldn't take them back.

Way to go Seun. Now he's going to think you're some angry fellow with no joy.

But aren't you? And why do you even care?

She dismissed the thoughts and looked sideways to find him already looking at her. He smiled and winked.

'There's always something to laugh about. It depends on which way you're looking.' *Says the pot to the kettle.* His subconscious chided him and he ignored it.

'It's a lady.' She suddenly said and returned his smile. There was no need to keep being defensive around this man. He felt harmless enough, he didn't seem to have much baggage and most importantly, he didn't know her.

Confusion clouded his features and she quickly clarified. 'The person I came to see I mean. She's a lady.'

'Oh.'

'Yup. But I've changed my mind. I'll call her when I get home.'

'Why?'

Could this guy get any nosier?

'I just...' She didn't know what to say and she really didn't want to lie.

He saved her just in time. Raising both hands in mock surrender, he gave her a wry smile. 'I know. It's none of my business.'

'No.' She started. 'I mean, yes. It's none of your business but like, it's kind of...complicated. She's not exactly a friend. It was supposed to be more of a business meeting.' She didn't understand what made her want to make him feel better. Hadn't she been badmouthing him in her head just a second ago? She mentally facepalmed.

'Hm, I understand. Impressions matter and all.'

'Yup.'

He nodded and observed her for a second. 'Do you need a ride?'

Her car was at the mechanic's and she would actually appreciate a ride. She had been using taxis for weeks and her budget was crying. But for one, she wasn't sure she was ready to be in an enclosed space alone with this guy; he made her feel things she wasn't ready to acknowledge just yet. And two, she knew he had already been there today for work. She could just book another ride.

'I have a car Frank.' She hoped that would end the conversation.

'Yes, I know.' He laughed. 'But, I saw you walk out of a taxi earlier so I assumed you didn't come with your car.'

'Oh. So you running into me wasn't a mistake? Stalker much?' She raised an eyebrow and tried to deflect her lie. It worked..

'Well technically, you ran into me madam.' He stopped and gave her a pointed look. 'I came out with an umbrella to help when I saw how you were struggling and you ran into me.' He said the 'you ran into me' in a matter-of-fact tone.

Now she just felt stupid. 'Oh.'

'Yeah.'

'I'm sorry. Well, thanks for the offer. But I'll just call another ride.'

He looked like he was about to say something else but he decided against it and nodded. 'Alright then.'

'Thanks for the jacket.' She took it off and handed it back to him. An awkward silence fell over them and she felt even more stupid. Her shirt was still drenched. And she secretly hoped he'd push so she could say yes since he insisted. He didn't.

'You're welcome.' He took the jacket and started down the corridor. Her disappointment grew.

***

She thought for a second before making her decision. 'Hey Frank!' She called him back.

'Hm?' He turned and it all looked so dramatic.

She wanted to laugh out loud at how much the whole thing reminded her of a movie scene but she thought against it. 'Let's go.'

He broke into a wide grin and she felt like she had just handed a child the sweet that a bully snatched from him. She felt good. Ignoring the warning sirens in her head that this was a bad idea, she caught up with him and slipped her hands in his. He handed her the jacket back and they left together.

The car ride was relatively quiet as they were both lost in their thoughts. Seun wasn't sure what had pushed her to agree to this but it felt so right so she went with the flow. Of course, there was the undeniable attraction she felt towards him. There was that.

He wasn't innocent either, she saw it in his eyes. And even though she now knew he was a single parent like herself, she could tell his life didn't have much else in common with hers. And there might be a baby mama or ex-wife somewhere in the picture just waiting to pop this bubble she was in.

'We're here.' Frank's voice pulled her out of her reverie and she looked up at him.

'Right. Thanks for the ride.'

'You're welcome.' He leaned back in his chair and studied her.

'Alright. See you around.' She nodded and started to get out of the car.

'Seun.' He called her back. How on earth did her name manage to sound better on his lips than it sounded from hers?

'Yes?'

He had been calling to ask her for his jacket but then he thought against it. He wanted to have a reason to talk to her again later plus now was as good a time as any to get her number since he hadn't gotten around to collecting it from Christian.

'Can I have your number?' He put his tongue in his cheeks and waited for her to tell him no.

'Oh so you think because you gave me one ride, I have to give you my number. Why am I surprised? All men are the same.' She went off at him and he just stared. He had been expecting a no but now she was just being...irrational.

She burst out laughing and he got even more confused.

'I'm joking. But ah, the look on your face was so priceless.'

He sighed and facepalmed. 'I for say o.' He laughed too.

She called her number out to him and gave a slight wave as he drove off. As soon as his car left the gates, it hit her. His jacket was still with her. Oh crap.▯

Chapter 5

Surulere, Lagos, Nigeria | August 2019 |

Frank had been avoiding reading the book since the last time.

'...don't stop reading when it gets too painful because it will.'

He remembered the words on the book's back cover and he struggled within himself. He'd reached for it several times in the past few weeks but he just couldn't get himself to open it.

Seeing it all the time on his bedside table made it even harder. So he moved it into a drawer and forgot about it. That was, of course, until today. Today was Saturday and he had lots of time on his hands this weekend. He had closed all the deals for the sale of his tech company and he didn't have many things on his mind. There was nothing to distract him and he found himself wanting to reach for the book.

'Just be a little kinder, show a little more humility and love a little more.' The words rang in his head and he savored them for a second before making a decision. He'd continue reading it; but not now.

Now, he was in a state of dilemma.

He blinked and switched to the next thing on his mind. Seun. He wanted to call her and hear her voice. He had become inexplicably drawn to her and he didn't know exactly how to feel about it.

As quickly as the idea to call her popped into his head, he dismissed it. His jacket was still with her and he concluded that whenever he mustered up the courage, he'd call. She was probably already wondering why he'd collected her number if he didn't plan to use it.

'I'm not ready for this.' He muttered to his empty room. It was becoming a habit.

Pushing the thoughts to the back of his head, he decided to take a power nap. Maybe then, he'd stop thinking about it. Just as he started to drift off to sleep, Nora barged into his room.

'Daddy!'

He fought off the urge to groan and gave her the best smile he could muster. 'Hey baby.'

Opening his arms wide, he caught her as she jumped into his bed. 'Easy there. You don't want to break your old man's back do you?'

She broke into peals of laughter. 'Old.' She scrunched up her face and put her hands on her chin, thinking for a second. 'I don't think you're old daddy. You're...' She counted with her fingers. 'Thirty.'

'Haha. Close enough. I'm thirty one.'

'Yes. Thirty one. Okay, that is a little old. Hehe.'

'Yeah it is. And soon it'll be your turn to be an adult and take care of me.' He tapped her nose and winked.

'I'll take care of you daddy.' She smiled and hugged him.

'Speaking of care and rest and all of that, why are you not taking a nap like I told you to young lady? You can't bribe me with a hug o.'

She shook her head. 'I couldn't sleep. I was dreaming of mummy again.'

He sighed and rubbed his temples. He couldn't scold her for that. *God help me. We've been through this already. Multiple times.*

'Baby I told you. Mummy's sleeping for a very very long time now.'

'But why can't she sleep here, with us?' Nora pestered.

'She's with God now Nora. And that's a better place for her.'

'Well, I want to be in a better place too. With mummy. Everyone in school has a mummy.' She was starting to cry and he gathered her close, praying for strength to hold in his own tears.

'No baby. It doesn't work like that. Something bad happened to her and it was really painful. But God took her to be with Him so that she'd be at peace.'

She nodded slowly and looked up at him with wide, innocent eyes. 'I miss her.'

'Me too baby. Me too.' He hugged her again and shut his eyes tight. His tears flowed freely now and he didn't try to stop them. He missed her so much.

'Daddy don't cry.' She licked her lips and pinned him with a stare, reaching up to wipe his tears. 'You said she's in a better place right?'

'Yes.' His breath caught in his throat and he tried not to think of what he'd do if he ever lost Nora too. Never.

'I cannot remember her very well daddy.'

She said it so honestly but it broke his heart. She had only been four going on five when Laura died. Her memories were fading and he battled in his mind to come to terms with it.

'Don't worry. I remember her well enough for the two of us.' He tried for a smile and she gave him a sad smile in return.

'Okay. But...' She paused. 'Do we ever get to see her again?'

'Yes. We'll get to see her, and God, and your baby brother too, and we'll all be in heaven; happy. And a family again.' He smiled through his tears. This time, a genuine one.

'Hm.'

'But that's a long long time away. So until then, we have to love God and love others so that we'll go to heaven and see mummy again.'

'I will.'

Ask her about Seun.

The nudge in his heart was so strong he knew it was God leading him. He hesitated for a second before asking her.

'Including Aunty Seun.' He gave her a knowing look and she looked down. 'Have you forgiven her? Do you love her now?'

She pursed her lips and said nothing.

'Hm Nora. What are you saying?' He nudged her gently and raised her head so her eyes were level with his.

'I-I-I think so.'

'You think so?' He squinted his eyes at her playfully. 'What does the bible say in Ephesians 4:32 Nora?'

'"Be kind to each other and forgive.' She muttered.

'Good girl. And why is that?'

She looked down and played with her fingers. 'Because God forgave us through Jesus."

'Exactly. So, do you still think so or are you sure?' She looked at him and nodded. 'Huh?' He smiled at her and an idea popped into his head. 'I can't hear you.' He tipped her unto the bed and tickled her. She giggled and screamed, trying to push his hands away without success.

'Daddy!' She hiccuped. 'Please. Okay, okay, yes yes yes.'

'Yes what?'

'I forgive her.' She mumbled.

'Good girl.' He gave her a high five and placed a kiss on her head.

Leaning back into his pillows, he got a full view of her face and what he saw there worried him. 'What's wrong baby? What are you thinking of?'

'It's Aunty Seun.'

Not again. 'What about her?'

'I saw her in my dream too.'

He sat up and his mouth hung open momentarily. That was definitely not what he was expecting. 'You did what?'

'I saw her in my dream.'

She folded and unfolded her little hands as she spoke, obviously nervous. He held her hand in his and squeezed a bit, hoping to help her relax. Laura always did that and holding her hands used to calm her. It worked.

'And?' He prompted.

'And she was walking with mummy. They spoke but I didn't hear what they said. Mummy hugged her and I tried to go to them but I couldn't move.' She was crying again.

'It's okay baby.' He drew her closer, placing her head on his chest and patting her back gently. 'So what happened next?'

'Mummy walked away, then Aunty Seun saw me. She wanted to hold my hand but I ran away from her.' She heaved and blew her nose loudly, soaking up his light t-shirt with her tears.

'It's okay.' He kept crooning to her till she fell asleep on him.

Normally, he'd carry her to her room once she slept off but he didn't want her waking up to an empty room and bursting into tears again. Plus, he sensed that this particular dream had really shaken her up.

She usually dreamt of memories she had of her mum and they were mostly good until she woke up and realized it was only a dream. No mummy. Then the waterworks came. But even those dreams had become short and far in-between.

This one was different. There had been another woman in the dream. And not just any woman, but the one he was falling for. Maybe God was trying to tell him something.

Lord is this a sign? Are you telling me she's no good for me or are you saying she's what I need, what we need?

Even as he prayed, a peace came over him.

Just let me lead.

He sighed and lay Nora properly on the bed beside him. He tucked the blanket in properly around her and her calm sleeping face was the exact contrast to what it'd been earlier: animated, sad and worried.

Placing another kiss on her head, he settled in to sleep too, the book, momentarily forgotten.

Just let me lead.

Chapter 6

Apapa, Lagos, Nigeria | August 2019 |

Seun paced the Home's grounds, lost in thought.

Taking a seat on the park bench, she took in a deep breath and reminisced on her life in the past few years. Many things had changed, some bad but mostly good. She was in a better place than she'd been and she had Temi to thank for it.

She tried not to think too much about Dozie but he always found a way to sneak back into her thoughts. Like now, she stared at her phone screen like it had suddenly grown a horn.

And all for what? A simple call.

No.

It'd have been a simple call if Dozie hadn't made her terrified of picking calls. Whenever she stopped picking his calls, he always tried to trick her into picking them by using an unknown number.

She let it ring for a few minutes before thinking of how absurd the whole thing was. Maybe she was just being dramatic. He hadn't tried to reach her since the last time she'd seen him, when they'd had sex while Uzi slept.

She was ashamed of the whole 'incident'. Incident. That's what she chose to see it as, and she wished to wipe it off her memory completely.

Dozie made her skin crawl yet her body responded to him in ways she couldn't explain. She closed her eyes and exhaled. He wasn't even here and he was getting under her skin. Opening her eyes, she reached for the phone and picked it. If it was Dozie, she'd block him. Again.

'Hello.'

Frank's clear voice sounded through the receiver and an inexplicable sense of calm came over her.

'Hi.' Her voice came out shaky and unsure.

'Seun, it's me, Frank.' He picked up on her tone and introduced himself.

As if she'd forget his voice.

'I thought you'd never call.' It was out of her mouth before she could think and she bit her lips. She hadn't meant to say that.

'Hm, is that a thinly veiled I-missed-you?' He joked.

'No. It's a very straightforward I-thought-you'd-never-call.' She smiled for a second, and then looked at the phone quickly, like she was scared he'd somehow know she was smiling.

Rolling her eyes at how ridiculous the act had been, she held the phone between her shoulder and ears as she opened the door and entered her house. It was getting chilly outside.

'Touche.'

The line went quiet and she almost thought he had dropped the call till she heard him sigh.

'Hello?' It surprised her how much disappointment had already built up in her mind in the few moments she thought he'd cut the call on her.

'I'm here.' He said softly.

'Ha. I thought I lost you for a second.'

'I'm here.' He said again. There was no assumption in his tone and his words gave her a sense of protection that she tried not to hold on to. It felt strange and unfamiliar coming from a man.

He seemed to be deciding whether or not to say what he wanted to. And that sole fact made her want to hear it so desperately, she couldn't understand why.

'What's on your mind?'

'You.' He said it simply. No holdbacks. And it unnerved her.

'Huh?'

'You are on my mind.' He repeated.

'Really?' She didn't know what else to say.

'Yes. You've been on my mind since the first day I met you.'

Asides the fact that he was being incredibly cheesy and corny, warning bells rang in her head and she mentally withdrew.

'Oh-kay.'

'I'm serious o. I mean, I can't even give a good reason for calling. I just knew I wanted to talk to you, maybe even see you. I like you.'

It couldn't get more straightforward than that. His words made her sit up straighter and she blurted the first thing that came to mind. 'Hm. I'm not sure your mother's daughter will be too happy to hear that.'

He went silent again and this time she was sure he'd cut the call. *Way to go*, she chided herself. *You've scared him away with your big mouth. Happy now?*

'She's...' He cleared his throat.

So he hadn't cut the call. She waited to hear what he had to say. Probably give some silly excuse.

'She died. In a plane crash. Two years ago.'

As the words sank in, Seun cringed and face palmed. His wife was dead and she had just tactlessly made everything awkward. She'd probably have known if she'd asked Temi about him like she planned to.

But she hadn't, because she didn't want to give her any false hope about them having a thing. Temi was always trying to match-make her with 'eligible' men and it was so tiring even though she meant well.

Now I've made a fool of myself. And ruined the vibe. Just great.

'I'm sorry. I didn't know.'

'It's fine. I know you didn't know.'

The tension hung in the air and Seun wished she'd just gone with the flow. She liked him too anyway and for the first time in a while, she was actually feeling comfortable talking to a new guy. Even if this new guy had some baggage.

Baggage just like yours, her subconscious reminded her.

'About that date...' She started.

'What date?'

His words registered in her head and she regretted bringing it up. 'I thought you said you wanted to see me. I mean, I a-assumed you meant like a d-d-d...' She stammered and she wanted the ground to open and swallow her.

'Date?' He offered.

He sounded like he was holding back laughter and something told her he was. How much more embarrassing could this get?

'Yes.' She said limply.

'Relax Seun. That is what I meant. I just wanted to hear you say it.'

She breathed a sigh of relief. She didn't even care if he heard her at this point.

'Haha. You got me there.' Smiling in spite of herself, she asked him, 'So, where did you have in mind?'

'Well, I was hoping to ask if you had any ideas. I'm actually out of experience. I was married for almost five years you know.'

She tried to ignore the fears that lingered in her head at the talk of marriage. Plus, how old was he exactly? She attempted some mental calculations and her fears grew. A young daughter, over four years of marriage and two years plus of widowerhood.

She wasn't that old but she'd had a share of life problems than most people experienced in their lifetime and her own baggage was everything but pretty. She didn't need more.

In his defense though, his baggage seems clean.

Sighing, she resolved to give it a shot.

'How about a beach outing? I haven't been there in years.' The last time she had actually been on one was when there was still a sense of sanity in her home, as a child. She'd gone with her parents and that was one of the only happy memories she had with them.

'A beach then. How does, uh, Eti-okun Bay sound?'

'Sounds good to me.'

'It's a date then.'

'Yup.' She was already very deep in thought.

'So next weekend?'

'Yes, next weekend is fine.' Her reply was half-hearted but Frank didn't notice.

'See you then.'

'See you.' She replied in an almost whisper and ended the call.

Holding the phone to her chest, she rested her head on a throw pillow and let out the breath she didn't know she'd been holding. She took off her glasses and wiped the sweat on her face despite the air conditioner blowing from the corner of the room. Her heart wouldn't stop beating fast and she could feel herself falling for this man; hard and fast.

She was scared.

Married. The word haunted her thoughts long after the call and she wondered for the hundredth time if she had done the right thing by agreeing to go on a date.□

Chapter 7

Surulere, Lagos, Nigeria | August 2019 |

Frank was at his wit's end. He'd planned with Nora's nanny for Saturday to give room for his date with Seun. But the lady's husband just called to cancel saying she was sick.

Something told him there was nothing wrong with Aunty Kiki as Nora fondly called her. Her husband probably just wanted some me-time with her and as much as he wanted to be pissed, he understood. Problem was, now he needed to make new plans for Nora and he didn't know what to do. Either he found someone to keep Nora with or he called to cancel.

You don't even want to go and you know it. This is the perfect excuse.

The voice haunted his thoughts and he shook his head to clear it. Of course, he wanted to go on the date with Seun. He liked her. But he'd been feeling like a piece of trash since he asked her out.

Like a fraud. A cheat.

Would Laura hate him now?

Laura's dead Frank.

The thought made him clench his jaw. The more he thought about it, the worse he felt.

Am I moving on too early Lord? Am I even ready for this?

He scratched his beard and stared at his call log. If he called to cancel, he'd feel like a piece of trash and if he didn't call to cancel, he'd still feel like a piece of trash. He was torn.

He thought of Christian but quickly crossed him off the list. He was visiting his wife at her MBA school and wouldn't be back in Nigeria for weeks. Taiwo and Karen were off the table too because they had their hands full with moving into their new house.

Basically, all the people who could help were booed up and un-available. It struck him again how lonely he was and he sighed deeply.

You need to start moving on. It's what she'd want.

Sometimes he wondered if he'd done the right thing by selling his company. But frankly, it reminded him too much of Laura and it had also became quite boring for him. The more he'd held on to it, the more trapped he'd felt. But a few times like this, loneliness ate at him and he wished he had something doing.

No regrets, he chided himself. Sighing again, he focused on the issue at hand.

Another option was to take Nora on the date. He laughed at the absurdity of the thought. She'd have a fit and Seun would definitely find out about the incident of how they really met one way or the other. He could foresee a disaster.

A thought popped into his head and he suddenly felt so relieved. He'd take Nora to stay with Temi and Uzi. Problem solved.

Except...the children hated each other. But then again, they were children, they'd have to get over it sooner or later and now was as good a time as any. Plus, they could play with other kids too.

He adored Uzi almost as much as he cared about the boy's mother and he kept his fingers crossed about the date.

Please don't let this be a mistake Lord.

***

Her hands were crossed over her chest and she tilted her chin defiantly as she stared out the window. The car ride was incredibly tense and Frank kept stealing glances at her.

He knew she'd rather be anywhere else than in this car with him, on the way to drop her off with Temi and Uzi so he could go on a date with the boy's mother.

'Why do I have to come? What about Aunty Kiki?'

'I told you baby. She's sick and can't make it.' He was seriously starting to wonder if he was in his right mind for doing this.

'Hm, you mean she's strong.' She said it so matter-of-factly and a smile stole across his face.

She had started to catch on to the Nigerian way of saying the opposite of a bad thing as a manner of speaking good things into existence. It always made him laugh. 'Yes Nora, she's strong.'

'I wish Uncle Christian was around.'

'Me too baby. But remember, you said you'd try to like her.'

She went silent. And although it bothered him that she was having such a hard time forgiving for the first time since ever, he was content that at least she'd stopped complaining.

His relief was short lived though because her next question knocked the air out of him.

'Daddy. What is a date?'

He coughed.

'Bless you Daddy.'

'Thank you.' He blinked rapidly and tried to gather his thoughts. '*So...*'

God, this child is persistent.

'Yes. Well, a date is what two adults who like each other go on.' He bit his tongue and waited. He didn't have to wait long.

'Why?'

'So that they can get to know each other more.'

'Are you going to marry her?' This time, he could swear he actually stopped breathing for a few seconds. Why was a seven year old this intelligent? And more importantly, how was he supposed to answer that?

'My friend told me that his mummy and daddy go on dates. He said that they told him that they used to go on dates before they married. And that they still go now that they're married. And it's because they love each other.' She looked at him now. 'Do you love her?'

Now he wanted to enter the ground. He didn't know what to say. But he'd have loved to give Nora's friend a piece of his mind. What on earth did kids of these days not know? What happened to talking about Caprisonnes and toys?

'What about mummy?' She sounded close to tears and he mentally kicked himself.

God help me. Give me the right words to say.

He had to park for this one. Pulling up to the side of the road, he turned to Nora and held her both hands to calm her.

'I don't know if I love her yet baby. But I know I like her and I'd like to get to know her.'

'And what of mummy and me?' Her eyes were filled with tears now.

'I love you guys very much and that will never change. But mummy is with God and we won't see her for a very very long time. She would want us to be happy. She'd want us to move on.'

'Why? I don't want to move on. And I don't like Aunty Seun.' She kept crying and he held her close, patting her back.

He considered calling Seun to cancel but they were almost there and he started to think of how things might be if they actually got in a proper relationship. He wasn't one for playing games. Ever. And he wasn't trying to have a fling with her. He wanted something real, that could lead to marriage.

And even if he didn't know much, he knew there'd be times when Nora might unintentionally manipulate him into making the wrong decision about his relationship with Seun. Or with any other woman for that matter. He had to learn to stand his ground early enough. He knew that much.

'It will be fine baby. God will help us do the right thing.' It broke his heart that his seven year old had been exposed to so much pain too early in her life, making her think years above her age. She deserved her childhood and he was trying his possible best to make it happy for her. Sometimes, he just felt so powerless. Like now.

'Okay.' She stared at him for a long second before scooting back into her seat and pulling her seat belt on. He was shocked at how at peace she suddenly looked but he wasn't complaining. In actual fact, he was thankful for it. 'Let's go.'

Thank you God.

They rode the rest of the way to the Home in companionable silence and he hoped that the date would be well worth it. He was letting this woman not only into his heart and life, but that of his daughter. He was taking a risk and he hoped to God that it was a right one.

***

Apapa, Lagos, Nigeria | August 2019 |

'You look good.' Frank turned to Seun and gave her a quick wink.

'Thank you. You don't look half bad yourself.' She smiled and patted him lightly on the arm.

'Trust you to give a half compliment.' He teased. 'What's wrong with saying you look good too? Or better still, you look rather smashing today Frank. If I stare at you too long, I might actually start to sweat or melt. Yes, because you're that hot.'

She laughed at the straight face he had on as he spoke. Turning to face him as much as she could within the seat belt's constraints, she cleared her throat and faked an accent. 'Why yes my Lord, you do look rather smashing!'

They both laughed and whatever tension they'd felt earlier seemed to have eased.

He was dressed in shorts and a Hawaiin-style shirt that he left unbuttoned to reveal well-formed muscles beneath a grey vest. Seun wore a plain sleeveless top and cargo pants.

'So tell me Seun, I know you work with Christian and all. But I'm curious. What else do you do?' He asked, careful to avoid sounding demeaning.

'Ha. I know it's not much of a career. But I am...sort-of a writer.' She answered. She intentionally answered vaguely.

Vaguely? That was a half lie madam.

It wasn't exactly like she could tell him she was an anonymous writer with a pen name. That'd just give rise to a string of questions she wasn't willing to answer. Not now. Probably never.

'Hm. So, like a blogger or freelance writer? Or an author?' He looked at her briefly. 'Aspiring maybe?'

'Something like that.' She cleared her throat and squirmed in her seat. Aspiring? *You have no idea,* she thought. Not liking the line of the conversation, she decided to turn the tables.

'So Frank, enough about me. What about you? What's your big story?'

'Ha, well played ma.' A sheepish smile crept into her face. 'Well, I am an app developer. I worked in tech for a while before launching my own app, a music streaming and talent mining app. It did well, got funding and expanded to Canada with over five hundred thousand users. We had even better projections for the future.'

'Wow. Sounds like fun and money.' Looking at him mischievously, she added, 'But why had? Are you unemployed now?'

'Haha! No. But you're right, it was really fun at first and the money was good. But I got fed up after a while. I sold the company last year.'

'Hm.' She simply said, wondering what could have been so tiring about being CEO that made him quit. It felt like there was more to the story but she didn't pry. If she was being completely honest, he'd revealed way more than she'd have in his shoes. She had literally lied about her career. Shaking off the feeling of guilt that was quickly settling over her, she shot him a smile. 'Perks of being your own boss I guess.'

He grinned widely. 'It's not as glamorous as it sounds.'

'Says the former CEO,' she pointed at herself, 'to the bloody nine-to-five employee.' Seun rolled her eyes and he shook his head, laughing quietly.

It didn't take them long to get to the jetty and Frank pulled into a make-shit parking lot where several area boys stood around hustling N200 and N500 notes from people.

He handed the young boy hanging around their car a N1000 note and Seun smiled at him. Calling the boy over to her window, she slipped an extra N500 note into his hands and waved him off when he started to prostrate.

'Hm, what was that for?' He was curious about her.

'There's enough suffering and poverty in the world. If these boys had a choice, they wouldn't be here you know. And I know I may not be able to change the world but I've seen and experienced enough pain to know that one little act can mean the world to someone else in a moment in time.'

He smiled knowingly and squeezed her hands lightly. 'You're a good person.'

She laughed dryly. If only he knew. 'You have no idea.'

Wondering at her words, he stepped out of the car and hurried to open the door for her.

She thanked him and looked around. For the first time since they got there, it hit her that they were at a jetty and not the actual beach. As in, they would have to take a boat to where they were going. Panic filled her and she grabbed Frank's hand.

'We're getting on a boat?'

'Yes.' He saw the fear in her eyes. 'Wait, you've never been to Eti-Okun have you?'

'Actually, I've only ever been to one beach and I don't even re-member the name, it was so long ago.' She blinked quickly and struggled to hold back tears.

'That explains it.'

'Hm hm.'

***

Eti-Okun, Victoria Island, Lagos, Nigeria | August 2019 |

'Are you okay Seun?' She didn't realize she had stopped walking till Frank walked back towards her and stood right in front of her. A lone tear escaped her eyes and she wanted to hide from his probing gaze.

'Seun?' He called again. This time he lifted his hands to her face and took off her glasses, wiping her wet cheeks.

It took every ounce of self control in her not to lean into his touch. 'Hm, I'm fine.' She looked down. 'It's just uh, the ocean air getting to me.' She spoke too quickly and it was obvious she was lying.

As if to support her lie, a cool breeze washed over them in waves. How ironic.

It was both the fear of taking a boat and her childhood memories that were getting to her. She collected her glasses and put them back on.

'Seun, I didn't know you didn't know that we needed to take a boat to Eti-Okun. If I did, I'd have mentioned it. It's nothing to be afraid of. In fact, it's quite the adventure. But if you're too uncomfortable with it, just say the word and we'll leave right now. But please for heaven's sake, don't cry.'

She nodded and smiled up at him. 'I told you. It was just the breeze.'

He wanted to tell her he didn't believe her but thought better against it. He knew she would never admit it.

Yes, she was terrified to her bones and nostalgic feelings made her want to hide under a blanket. But she wanted to experience this and she also didn't want to disappoint him. So she threw on her poker face and willed her legs to move.

Taking his hand, she fell into step beside him and let him lead her to the speedboats.

As they got on a boat, he kept stealing worried glances at her and her fingers curled tighter around his hand. She squeezed her eyes shut and counted under her breath. She knew her grip on his hand had to hurt but it was the only way she could stop her hands from shaking as the boat swayed from side to side on the water.

Everything in her screamed at her to run but having him around eased her fears a little and even though her heartbeat had become way faster, his other hand gently patting her back calmed her.

'Are you sure you want to do this? I know I said it's just fifteen minutes but I can't help but feel like I'm leading a lamb to the slaughter.'

She opened her eyes and smiled feebly at him. 'I'm sure. Sometimes in life, you just need to face your fears head on to realize that they're too small to hold you back.'

'Oshey bars!' Their throaty laughter filled the air and other passengers stared at them. Some smiled while a few shot them dirty looks. They didn't care. The minutes passed quickly and they reached the beach in no time.

When they got off the speedboat, Seun's legs shook a bit and she leaned into Frank for support before finally finding her footing.

'Whoooooooooooooooooooop! I did it!' She pulled out of his hold and jumped, punching into the air. After the initial shock, Frank laughed along with her. This time, everyone had dispersed to different areas of the beach and were too busy with their own business to be disturbed by their laughter.

Her joy was contagious and Frank wondered where the slightly uptight, standoffish Seun was. Here before him was a relaxed, playful, happy even, version of her. He definitely liked this Seun better.

As soon as they got into their rented cabana with some food, Seun put her glasses in her bag and pulled on some shades. She handed him a spare. 'I figured you didn't bring one.'

'You're right. I didn't.' He smiled and took it from her.

'Oldie.' She joked.

'Says the lady who hasn't been to a beach in ages.' He fired back.

She liked that he didn't take offense at the age joke. 'Touche.'

From beneath her shades, she got to take a good look of his face without getting noticed and she took her time. He looked amazing for a thirty plus and the man knew how to dress. But, she could see some stress on his face, like he was worried about something.

'Checking me out I see?' His words broke into her thoughts and she looked away in embarrassment.

How did he know?

'Don't even bother to deny it or ask me how I'm so sure. I am a masterpiece dear. Who wouldn't stare at a baby boy like me?' He flipped imaginary hair and pinned her with a look. She face-palmed. 'I know you're probably trying to get the whole beach experience thing to the T, but that's not your only reason for pulling on shades...while we're under a cabana, a literal shade.'

Her mouth hung open and he laughed.

'You are so full of yourself.' She muttered and crossed her arms. She didn't appreciate being caught in the act. She took off the shades.

'Oh relax darling, I don't mind.' He took off his shades too and winked. 'I was checking you out too.'

She huffed and looked back at him. The nerve of this guy. 'You think you're so smooth don't you? Please who's your darling?'

He threw his head back and laughed, a deep throaty laugh that reached his eyes. The worry lines had eased a bit.

'Please. I'm smoother than a new born baby's skin.' He patted his face and winked. 'Argue with the other person in this cabana.'

She rolled her eyes. 'There's no one here but us.'

'My point exactly.' He enjoyed teasing her, even at his own expense.

'Frank, these your dry jokes are getting too much. Should I be worried?' She poked him and chuckled as she watched him hold his stomach in over-dramatized 'pain'.

'That hurt you know?'

'What? The poke or my statement?' She was enjoying her time with him, her former fears about the date felt like they'd been light years ago.

'Both.' They laughed.

The day went by pretty fast. He teased her about being a scaredy cat when she refused to get on a speedboat. They tried coconut water, bought beach hats and overpriced bracelets, played a bit around the water and took a million pictures. They even picked shells at Frank's insistence.

'It's an unspoken beach rule.' He'd said just as he took off his shirt and handed it to her.

Grateful, she wrapped the shirt around her and rubbed her arms. The air had gone chilly. 'Really?'

'Yes. And don't worry about what we'll use them for. Nora will be more than happy to add it to her 'collection'. She has an entire stash and Uzi might like some too.'

'Haha, okay.'

In a heartbeat, he was in front of her. His face was so close she thought he was going to kiss her. Instead, he wrapped her in a hug and whispered. 'You're cold. This should help.'

The simple act warmed her heart as much as it sent electric jolts through her body. Their eyes met and Seun looked away quickly. Staring into his eyes would have her addressing feelings she wasn't quite ready for. Taking her hands, he'd placed them in his and rubbed till she felt better. The memory made her smile.

Frank was so much fun and when it was time to leave, she wished they could stay longer. The boat ride back was less dramatic and much more relaxing than the first one. They were on the road to the Home in no time.

Chapter 8

Surulere, Lagos, Nigeria | August 2019 |

Frank didn't get to ask Nora how her day went that night. She was asleep when they go

t back and he didn't want to wake her. While they prepared for church the next day, she didn't say a word and he started to feel jittery.

It's like a ticking time bomb in here Lord. Make it stop.

On their way back from church, he finally cracked and asked her.

'So, how was your day yesterday baby?'

'It was fine.'

He blinked.

'Really?'

'Yes.' She answered simply.

He wasn't convinced.

'Did anything interesting happen?'

'No.'

It didn't look like she planned on telling him anything else so he focused on his driving. He stopped by their usual ice-cream place before heading home. If he needed more information, he'd have to ask Temi. But he already did that. And she said everything went well. Typical of her to say. She never had a bad word to say about anyone.

Or maybe God will show me in a dream.

He chuckled at his own thoughts and looked at Nora quickly. She hadn't even noticed. She was staring out the window, as usual.

As soon as they got home, Nora went off to take a nap and he was left alone with his thoughts. He remembered the book he was supposed to be reading and brought it out from where he'd hidden it. After such a long time of putting it off, he felt it was time to continue reading and finally add more pieces to the puzzle...

***

Entry Three - August, 2018

They died today. I hate them and I hate myself.

Today is my fifteenth birthday you know. But they fought again and I don't even remember why.

I hate this. I want to die.

Okay so maybe not. I don't want to die. I just want the pain to end you know?

Well, let me tell you how they died. Today. On my birthday.

No. They didn't die together. But they kind of did.

The day started relatively well and I had a false sense of peace. But things started going downhill pretty quickly and I just knew something was coming.

By this time, I had already discovered another means of escape; my beloved headset. So I put it on the highest volume and listened to music in my room.

No one would ever have imagined that I was in a house with its roof on fire...literally.

Well, except the neighbors, they could hear. They always did. They have changed over the years but they are all the same to me. They all drink water and mind their businesses; no one ever mentions it and I am used to it. Their silence is deafening. Even after the accident, they all shook their heads and shed a few tears; no words.

Anyway, as I was saying, a loud bang interrupted my music and I jumped with a start, taking off the headset in one move. I flew off the bed and ran downstairs.

My beloved parents had taken the fight outside and it wasn't their first time doing it even though it was very rare.

I ran outside to a mob of people. They looked at me pitifully as I walked to the centre of the crowd.

There was a truck. And beside it, my dad's lifeless body. My mum stood there, motionless, staring at his body, in a pool of his own blood. He was dead.

I took in the whole scene for a few seconds and then passed out. I opened my eyes in a hospital bed.

✳✳✳

Entry Four - September, 2018

People think that only my dad died that day. And it makes me laugh. Not the happy, toothy kind, no. The bitter kind. I laugh because they don't know. They don't know that my mum died with him. And a piece of me too; everyday since then.

I'll explain.

Mummy has been forgetting impossible things for months now. At first, I thought it was just the trauma. It's what we all thought.

But as it got worse, her colleagues and friends started to notice.

With time, I started to identify a pattern. She usually had difficulty remembering names, forgetting stuff she read a second ago and misplacing valuable things.

At some point, she started struggling with planning for things that were so easy for her in the past. I mean, she even forgot my name a few times.

My mum, so self righteous and broken, was diagnosed with Alzheimer's two months ago.

***

Alzheimers.

The word sounded familiar but it felt like something only meant for the TV screens in foreign countries, straight out of Grey's Anatomy.

He couldn't even start to imagine how Tabitha had felt. Clenching his jaw, he closed the book and leaned back on his pillows. She'd been dead serious when she said the book would get painful. He'd known to expect some level of stress from reading the book but this was way above what he could have ever anticipated. If he felt like this just from reading the book, how on earth had Tabitha lived through this?

Pray for her.

Getting on his knees, he said a prayer for this total stranger. He prayed for healing, restoration and peace. As he rose to his feet, he felt God place in his heart to write her some fanmail. After searching for her author contact details on the book to no avail, he decided to write to her publisher and hoped it would get to her. The alternative was to drop a comment on her blog but he convinced himself that it would get lost in the sea of comments she got daily.

Bringing out a pen and paper he set out to write.

Dear Tabitha (I feel strongly that this is not your real name, but I have nothing else to go by),

I'm Frank, one of your recent fans. I think you are an amazing human and writer. I admire your style of writing. I have also gone through your blog and some of your posts on Instagram. You have such a beautiful soul and I admire your strength too.

Again, Tabitha you're amazing and I'm rooting for you. I started reading your book and it has made me think a lot.

I know that life is fickle and finite. It's really sad because we all want those we love to live forever, but they can't and that hurts. A few years ago, I lost my wife who was pregnant with our second child, so I understand this personally. It still feels so unreal sometimes and I occasionally feel like I've not processed this loss well enough. But I'm definitely way better than I was when it first happened and I've learned that the most important thing is to live in the present. As simple as that sounds, it becomes difficult because our human nature makes us fearful. The best we can do is try Tabitha.

I am sorry for what you've been through and I take it upon myself to apologize for all these people who hurt you. But I'd like to share something with you and please don't write it off too quickly. This is what helped me heal and start to find peace and the strength to raise my daughter alone these past few years. My faith in God.

'Throw all your anxiety onto him, because he cares about you.' - 1 Peter□ □5:7□

I am praying for you and I hope you give Him a chance to come into your life and do His healing work. You can start out by buying a bible and reading it with an open heart. If you don't mind also, here's my number if you'd like to talk: 080XXXXXXXX.

Love, Frank.

Before he could talk himself out of it, he typed it out and emailed it to the author email address he found on the book. He left an instruction for it to be forwarded to Tabitha, hoping that if she didn't handle the email account herself, whoever did would do just that.

It'd stand a better chance of reaching her than trying to send an email to the email address he found on her publisher's website. They probably got tons of cold call manuscripts in that email and his fan mail might get lost in the frenzy.

'What now Lord?' He asked aloud.

Now, you wait.

***

Maryland, Lagos, Nigeria | September 2019 |

Seun replied to comments on her blog. She didn't dwell on any for too long as they hadn't held any particular appeal to her for weeks now. Next, she browsed through her author emails. Several promotions, a work mail from Christian and...something caught her eye. An email from her editor, Mrs. Dede.

TV Interview Invite for Tabitha the Anon: An Exclusive.

She stared at it briefly before deleting it. She quickly moved on to other things. No way she was going to grant a TV interview, even if it was with CNN. She wasn't ready to show herself to the world yet and she probably would never be ready.

For the steady paychecks, she was thankful. But any 'publicity' stuff irked her. The best she could do was sign hard copies before they went out. But no interviews. No exhibitions. No tours. No radio. No podcasts and definitely no TV.

Another email caught her eye and this one she opened. It was some fan mail and she concluded that she could attend to it later. As she moved to close it and add it to her tasks, the name she saw made her stop. Frank. She knew it was him even before opening it.

She felt her heart rate increase as she read through with laser focus. The letter melted her heart but she couldn't call him like he wanted. He'd definitely find her out and she was still too scared to share that part of her life with him.

Plus, he'd mentioned loads of churchy stuff. It sounded pretty appealing but she wasn't sure yet. Temi believed in him, Frank believed. Maybe she'd consider it soon. They both said it gave them peace. And that's one thing she didn't have. Peace. Even though she was a 'Christian', she didn't believe that by simply believing, all your problems went away.

Next she checked her work email. Quickly replying Christian's mail about new book arrivals, she closed the email tab and scanned through Instagram. The first post she saw reminded her of Frank: What's your ideal first date location?

Speaking of first dates, she couldn't stop thinking about her first date with Frank. They'd gone out a few more times after the beach and she liked him more with each passing day. It was surreal and unbelievable.

Dozie hardly ever crossed her mind these days and she was really glad that Frank adored Uzi. She had noticed that Nora never really spoke to her but she tried to attribute it to her nature. Maybe she was just not a talkative child.

No. She doesn't like you.

Sighing, she kept scrolling.

Maybe she'll like me with time. She probably just misses her mum.

Yeah right.

Curiosity got the better of her and she searched for Frank Olu-muyiwa. It didn't take her long to find his profile. His bio simply read: God first, Father, Lover. Something felt missing in the bio. It finally clicked. Husband was probably a prominent part of his bio before he lost his wife. Frank was definitely the kind of man to do that, add his marital status to his bio because he held family in such high esteem. He had only a few pictures on there but they seemed to sum up his person very wholly. Some pictures of Nora, one of him and two others; a beautiful woman she didn't know. Obviously his wife.

Late wife.

Right.

The woman was smiling and looked happy; she had very striking features with a defined jawline and piercing eyes. Something in her eyes struck Seun and she liked her instantly. And she had a strong feeling that they'd have been really good friends if she'd ever met her in real life. She felt a slight feeling of envy about this woman.

Her aura was…peaceful; like someone who was confident in the life she was living. Or, well, the life she'd lived.

Her mind went back to Frank and unexpected tears filled her eyes. She liked him. A lot. But, fear's cold hands wrapped itself around her heart and she shrank back. She exited the app and dropped the phone like it had suddenly burned her.

You're not good enough for him. Look at his late wife. She is perfect. And you're everything but. You should back out now that it'll still be easy.

The words echoed in her mind. She buried her head in her hands and massaged slowly. As easily as the thoughts had flowed into her subconscious, she knew that it might be too late for her to step back. She already liked him too much.

If things didn't work between them, she'd be crushed. And everything in her screamed against the idea. She was drawn out of her thoughts as the store's door opened. A customer was here. Switching to work mode, she moved the thoughts to a side of her mind for later.

She didn't need this job but she had it before her blog and book blew up and became sensations. And she couldn't bring herself to leave just yet. Temi had helped her get it and she loved how it gave her access to lots of books. Plus, it gave her room to hold on to a sense of normalcy, despite her career success. It all still felt so surreal.

Few people in the world knew about her writing and if she quit now, she'd be 'unemployed' to the world. A single, unemployed mother. Typical Nigerian gossip fodder; the beginnings of a dramatic soap opera.

Chapter 9

Apapa, Lagos, Nigeria | September 2019 |

The ringing of her phone jerked her awake and she rubbed her eyes sleepily. Without looking at the caller, she picked.

'Hello.'

'Hello darling.' The hairs on her skin rose and goosebumps instantly formed. Dozie.

'Get off my phone Dozie.'

'Oh come on darling, stop pretending. You know you miss me. You miss feeling me inside you. You miss how I f*ck you. You...'

'Shut up! Just stop it!' She was shaking by now and she struggled to keep her grip on the phone. 'I do not miss your sorry self and I am never coming back to you so give it up already.'

'Come on. Tell me where you are. Let me give you what you know you really want.' He purred. His voice nauseated her.

'You have no idea what I want. And you are definitely not it. You have nothing I will ever want again!'

'You b*tch.' Gone was the fake sweet drawl he'd started with, he was in full beast mode now. 'You aren't worth anything. You think you're so much better than me now uhn? You are my leftover Seun and you'll surely come back to me. And you can't keep my son away from me.'

'Look Dozie. You don't own me and you definitely do not deserve to call Uzi your son. You told me to abort him, don't forget. And you don't get to come and pretend like you care about him now. Stay away from us Dozie. There's a court injunction, remember?'

'Seun...' His voice was menacing but she didn't let it stop her.

'Lose my number Dozie!' She cut the call and threw herself on the bed wondering how he'd managed to get her number again. Glancing at Uzi's bed in the corner, she was glad to see that he was still fast asleep. At least her raised voice hadn't woken him.

Picking her phone back up, she blocked Dozie's latest number and sighed heavily. Tears started to roll down her cheeks and she let them. Dozie's words had cut deep.

You aren't worth anything. You are my leftover.

Was he right?

He is right.

Temi kept telling her to resume her therapy sessions. It had been months since she last saw her therapist but she kept putting it off.

'I'm fine.' She cleaned her eyes and squared her shoulders. 'I am fine.'

She knew she was deceiving herself. Dozie was right. She did miss being loved. She missed him.

No you don't. You're letting him get to you.

Her therapist's advice rang in her head. 'When you feel anxious and think that someone is angry at you, dislikes you or that things are getting worse, ask yourself, "who told you that?" You will likely not have an answer or the person will be too insignificant in your life to matter and that will let you know that it's all in your mind.'

She nodded to the empty room and closed her eyes knowing she was not going to get any more sleep. Asides having a bucketload of sexual frustration she had no way to ease, she was actually considering Dozie's words. This was not good.

***

Apapa, Lagos, Nigeria | October 2019 |

Frank wanted to call Seun. They'd been dating for a while and he felt hopeful about their relationship. So it seemed only right to set up an outing with all four of them, him, Seun, Nora and Uzi.

Don't call her. Go there.

He did.

He saw her just as she walked towards the playing ground. Perfect. She saw his car and waved. He waved back.

'Hey beautiful.' He walked up to her and sat beside her on the bench before dropping a kiss on her cheeks.

'Hi.' She blushed and hugged him.

'So...'

'So, what are you doing here?'

He tapped his chest in mock hurt. 'Wow. So in other words, 'I don't want to see you Frank. Get out of here'.'

She laughed. 'No. I mean I wasn't expecting you. You didn't say you were coming.'

'Haha, I know. I was going to call but...well, here I am.'

'I'm happy you're here. I miss you.'

He stared at her for a long second. Then he smiled, and it reached his eyes. 'That's the first time you've said that to me.'

'Don't get used to it.' She rolled her eyes.

'Oh please, who are you deceiving?'

'Yen yen yen.' She smiled cheekily and eyed him playfully. But he noticed something else in her eyes. Fear? Worry? He wasn't sure. Since he couldn't quite place it, he concluded that it was all in his head and let it slide.

'You're in denial dear.' He replied before turning to her seriously. 'How's your writing going? We never really talk about it.'

She swallowed hard. 'It's going fine.' In her head, she had her fingers crossed, hoping he wouldn't pry further. He was always concerned about her work but she still wasn't ready to tell him more than what everyone else knew; she was a bookstore attendant and PA.

'Hm. I hope you let me see some of your works soon.' He gave her a small smile and dropped the subject. It obviously made her uncomfortable. Maybe she didn't think she was good enough.

'Anyway, I wanted to ask you something. I really think it might be time.'

'Time for?' *Oh no, is he going to propose?*

She held her breath. They barely knew each other.

His palms were getting sweaty but he stood his ground. He wasn't going to let nervousness get the better of him. Not today.

'Do you remember the day we first met?' He knew she didn't.

'Yes, at the bookstore. *Chai*, you were so fine.' She winked and tapped him playfully. *Whew, no proposal just yet.*

'Aww, she finally admits that she thinks I'm fine. Today is really my lucky day *o*. First, you admitted to missing me, now a compliment. Mama I made it.'

She tried to hide the smile that was creeping onto her face. '*Abeg abeg*, it's okay.'

'*Shior*. All this your hard guy won't get you anywhere madam. I know that deep down in your heart, you're a huge softie.' He stressed the huge and she couldn't help but laugh.

'Whatever.'

He took a deep breath. 'Actually, that wasn't the first day we met. And it's funny to me how you still don't remember.'

'I'm confused. Did we know each other before then?' She paused. 'Wait, let me rephrase that? Did you know me before then? Because I had definitely never met you before that day at the bookstore.'

She really had no idea.

'Don't be so sure about that.' His voice was low and quiet.

'Oh I'm sure. If I had seen you before, I'd remember. Your features are...memorable.' She bit her lip and looked away.

'Memorable hm? I know there's another compliment in there somewhere.' He wiggled his eyebrows and she tapped his arm playfully.

'Be serious *joh*.'

Sobering up, he asked her. 'You were at Taiwo and Karen's wedding right?' He tried to juggle her memory.

'Yes. Karen is Temi's daughter and my sister. I couldn't have missed it.' She squinted, wondering where this was going.

'Anything...memorable about the day?' He smiled and waited. He wanted her to remember on her own.

She shook her head slowly for a few seconds. Then her eyes went wide.

She remembered.

'No' She looked at him and tilted her head. 'No.' She was so embarrassed she could enter the ground. 'No.' She said again.

'Yes.' He nodded.

'Ah God. I'm so stupid.'

'Don't call yourself that.' He remained calm.

'But, urgh!' She face-palmed and stood up, pacing back and forth. 'Why haven't you ever said anything?'

'At first I found it really amusing and I actually waited for you to remember but when you didn't, it just became harder and harder to bring up.'

She kept pacing. 'So let me get this straight. Everybody knows but me. Temi, Tosan, the kids, you.'

'Now that you put it that way, it makes me feel really bad. I know I should have said something earlier. I'm really sorry. I honestly didn't think it was such a big deal.'

'You didn't think it was such a big deal?' By now, she had stopped in front of him and pinned him with a look.

He lifted his hands. 'Initially. I didn't think it was such a big deal initially.'

'No wonder she hates me. And she probably doesn't like Uzi very much either.' Sitting down, she held her head in her hands. She felt deflated. Gone was her angry, raging energy.

'She doesn't hate you. Or Uzi.' He placed a hand on her back and patted lightly.

She looked up. 'Don't patronise me Frank.'

'I mean, yes she's a bit distant. But she'll come around. We've talked about it.' That was a huge understatement but he was only trying to calm her nerves.

'You think?' For the first time since she found out, she felt a little hopeful.

'I know.' He squeezed her hand reassuringly and placed a kiss on the back. He hoped he was right.

'Look I'm sorry. I'm sorry for snapping at you and being dramatic. I should be the one apologizing to you. My conduct that day was inexcusable. I was drunk but the drinks weren't forced down my throat so yeah, I'm responsible for that.'

'It's okay, I've forgiven you already.'

She groaned. 'I owe Nora an apology too.'

'Yes. You do.'

'I'll do it. And I am really sorry again Frank. What must she think of me?' She sighed. 'I don't know how to feel.' It was more of a mutter than an actual statement but he heard.

'Don't beat yourself too much about it.'

'I'll try not to.' She stared into space, deep in thought. The events of the wedding played out in her head and she flinched. It had been really ugly. 'Thankfully, after that day, I felt so bad, I haven't touched a drop of alcohol since then and honestly, I don't think I will ever again.'

'Me too.' He smiled at her. 'It's a good choice.'

She smiled back. A small smile. But a smile anyway.

'And now, the important thing is the way forward.'

'Yes.'

'Speaking of the way forward, I actually came over to ask when you think we can have a double date, Nora and I, you and Uzi.'

She groaned. 'Oh boy.'

'Relax, it'll be fine.' He pulled her into a hug.

'I hope so. I really hope so.' She melted into the hug.

Chapter 10

Apapa, Lagos, Nigeria | October 2019 |

The double date had gone way better than she expected and she couldn't shake off the feeling of guilt days after. Nora was slowly warming up to her, Uzi and Frank literally adored each other and she was head over heels in love with Frank.

How is this man so perfect and lovable? I don't even deserve this. I don't fit in here.

Throughout the week, she opened and reopened his letter. Guilt was eating her up. She wanted to call and hear what he had to say about God's peace. She wanted to go to his house and tell him the truth.

You're a fraud Seun.

She shook her head. It didn't help.

Dozie is right. You are his leftover. You're not any better than him.

She wanted to stand up and go outside the room; get some fresh air. But she remained glued to the spot, unable to get up from the bed. She felt an anxiety attack coming on.

Oh come on now Seun, you know you want him. Don't you want Dozie to make love to you? Do you think anyone else can ever make you feel that good?

'Get out of my head!'

Are you sure this Frank guy even likes you like that? He's never even kissed you.

She was shaking uncontrollably now.

You're not good enough for him anyway and you know it. I mean, just look at his first wife. She was perfect. You can't fit into her shoes. Ever. You are filthy...

'Deep breaths. Deep breaths.' She murmured continuously as she clasped her both hands and attempted to still them.

Forget it. Once he knows you for who you truly are, he'll drop you like hot coals.

'One, two, three...' She counted till she felt her calm start to return.

Seun knew that she had put it off for too long and as the attack passed, she knew what she had to do. Call her therapist and book a session.

Now all that was left was the courage to do it.

***

Surulere, Lagos, Nigeria | October 2019 |

He remembered Nora's dream about Laura and Seun and he tried to pick the series of events apart. To understand it.

She'd had the dream a couple of times after that day and it was always progressive. First, she ran away. The next time, she only flinched when she came close and the last time, she let her hold her hand, even though she was unsure..

'It was nice. But I wish mummy didn't go.' That's what she had said the last time.

God, what are you saying to her? What are you saying to me; to us? Are you saying we are on the right track?

Even as he prayed and asked, it occurred to him that this might not be God's will. It might just be his mind telling him what he wanted to hear; thriving off whatever dreams Nora's trauma might be leading her to have.

So while some might say that Nora's dreams were sign enough, he needed a sign for himself. He was confused and lost and there was no knowing for sure if he was doing the right thing. For him and Nora. He needed a sign.

Just let me lead.

The words were becoming a constant in his thoughts. He wanted to do just that; let God lead. But it was easier said than done and he just wished he had more control over his life and how things played out. He had loved Laura with all his heart but he'd still lost her. He still loved her even. She was amazing and he missed her everyday.

But he knew he had to move on. And he wanted Seun to be in their future; his and Nora's. He wanted to build with her. It didn't matter to him that she had a child already. It would be very hyp-ocritical of him to think of writing her off because she had a son when he had a daughter too.

Of course, society was easier on single fathers than mothers regardless of how they came to be single parents but he wasn't one to pay much attention to what people said. With everything they'd shared, he hoped that she would start to open up to him more, especially about her past. He'd been pretty transparent about his; there was nothing to hide.

For Seun though, she was evasive about sharing details on her past and even her present life. It made him sad that she didn't seem to trust him enough. He'd bared his heart but she was hiding hers behind high walls, protecting it from the world.

He tried to be understanding but there was only so much he could take before breaking. Did she have something to hide?

He desired her body, he couldn't deny that. He was after all, a man who still had blood running through his veins. But his desire for her heart superseded his desire for her body. It was hard for him to keep himself from taking her into his arms and trying to do things with her even though he knew she'd probably let him.

He saw it in her eyes and it just made it all the more difficult to stick to his resolve.

But he also knew she had it rough with whoever the last man in her life was. He didn't want to scare her away or think that was all he was about. Her body. He was about her heart, her soul, her love and her body. And he believed that it would be more fulfilling and worth it if he did things right. God's way. He'd win her heart and her love. Then marry her. Before anything else.

You need to talk to her about this.

The thought made sense. He did need to talk to her and he would. Soon.

Another thing he wanted to tell her about was the book he was reading. He missed having someone to talk to about everything and anything. There was Nora of course, but there was only so much he could say to a seven year old.

He wanted to talk to Seun; about Tabitha and how he felt God leading him to reach out to her. But he didn't know how.

What if she gets jealous? You know how women are.

It would be ridiculous he knew. But then again, a lot of the things that women did and thought made no sense to him. Just like he was sure many things men did made women wonder about their sanity.

It had actually been weeks since he sent the letter to Tabitha and it irked him that she still hadn't replied. Maybe she didn't even get it. She probably got tons of fanmail.

He still felt strongly moved to tell Seun so he decided he'd do it after he finished reading the book. It was taking way longer than he'd even planned but at least it'd help him stall on telling her about it. It didn't feel like the right time yet.

So he kept reading...

***

Entry Five - October, 2018

Can you imagine? Mummy started to forget everything, one by one. She forgot the abuse too. She forgot daddy. And soon, she forgot me.

Do you know what that means? I am left with all the memories; the scars and nightmares. Alone.

I don't even try not to hate her. I hate her. And daddy too.

They made me like this and then left me to bear it all alone.

What child deserves this? What did I ever do wrong to deserve such a fate?

And to think those brainwashed christians always try to get me to become born again. Talking, oh cast all your cares on God.

God does not love anyone and He sure as hell doesn't love me. If he did, he wouldn't be letting me suffer like this. He wouldn't let so much evil and pain in the world.

He'd have saved me from this life by now.

***

Right. There was a reason why he hadn't picked up the book to read for such a long time. It was so sad and heartbreaking.

Why Lord? Why did she have to suffer like this?

Silence.

Closing his eyes, he tried to make sense of it.

'God doesn't wish evil on people and He does no evil. But people hurt people. And sometimes, bad things happen to good people. But it doesn't change the one fact. That God is good. All the time.' When his pastor said this in church one day, he'd been part of the people in the congregation with the whistles, chanting and screaming 'Preach Pastor! Yes! Glory to God! Rhema! Hallelujah!'

But there had also been people who had stayed, unmoving, as he said it, straightfaced and quiet. Melancholic. That was before Laura passed away. Now that he thought about it, they were probably the ones who understood the pain of losing a loved one or being hurt beyond words by fellow humans. People like him and Tabitha now.

He hadn't really understood then. But after Laura's passing, the reality of it became clearer to him.

God is good. All the time.

It wasn't easy to say or live by, but he was learning and he prayed daily that Tabitha would too. He prayed for her healing and for God to open her eyes.

Despite mourning Laura's death, he had some peace, knowing she was in God's bosom. Knowing that they would meet again at His feet. Could Tabitha say that for her parents? Likely not. But she was still alive, she still had life and room for salvation. And he prayed earnestly for the Holy Spirit to reach her.

Somehow he knew that this book, although painful, was some form of healing therapy for him. It stripped him bare to his soul and made him confront his deepest thoughts. His prayers for Tabitha were as much for him as they were for her.

He flipped the page and kept reading...

***

Entry Six - November 2018

My therapist says journaling is a good way to get things off my chest; she says it's healthy, so I will tell you. This one's a bit long so you might want to get comfortable...

When it all ended eventually, I told myself I would never be like them. Mostly, I would never be like her, my mother. But here I am, reliving her life.

I met Dozie at a party I shouldn't have been, with some friends I shouldn't have been keeping. But I didn't know any better. All I wanted was acceptance, and they gave me that. They also gave me things to help me forget my pain. They were my friends and we forgot our sad realities together, drowning in alcohol, weed and all manner of drugs. It was okay at first but soon, I became addicted.

From being my supplier, Dozie became my boyfriend. And when my mum's Alzheimer's progressed beyond a certain point, she was moved into a nursing home and I had all this freedom. I didn't know what to do with myself, my extended family was distant and Dozie was there.

In the beginning, he was sweet and caring. I easily fell in love with him. We rode waves of ecstasy together, experimented with our bodies and had the fun of our lives. Soon, I moved in with him. He was way older and had a weird, ominous and dangerous aura around him. He had some violent tendencies but I found it 'cool' and sexy. I was so stupid.

Some months into our relationship, he became more violent, emotionally and physically abusive. The first time he hit me, I was shocked. I was going to leave I promise you. But somehow, I didn't. And he kept hitting me, over and over again.

Then he apologised and I forgave him.

One day, it was stress. The next, provocation. Another, difficult clients. Different day, different story. He always had excuses for his anger and I ate them up, because I couldn't bear to be alone. I didn't want to think of how empty my life would be without him.

I tried so hard. But in the end, I was just like my mother. I was my mother. The apple doesn't fall far from the tree right?

I don't know how I managed to pull through school with all the craziness in my life but I did somehow. The day I found out I was pregnant was the day I caught him cheating. And apparently, he had been cheating all through our relationship with my so-called friends.

I cried my eyes out.

When I finally had the courage to tell him I was pregnant, he didn't bat an eyelid as he told me 'Don't you know what girls do Seun? Don't be silly please. Get rid of it.' He threw money at me and left the house.

I was seventeen.

***

Frank closed his eyes and groaned. His hands clenched into fists and he wished with everything in him that he could punch this Dozie guy. Not only had he taken advantage of a minor and gotten her pregnant, he had also gotten her hooked on drugs and abused her.

His head hurt. Still, he wanted to keep reading. He bookmarked the page he stopped, dropped the book on his bedside table and stared into space. He was almost done with the book and everything in him wanted to keep reading, to find out more about what happened. But he had to make some plans.

Nora's eight birthday was in a few days and for some reason, she wanted a party this year. Their apartment was too small to host a party and thankfully, Temi was more than willing to let them use the Home's park. Perfect.

He put his hands to his chest and tried to regulate his breath. He was so angry. If anyone did that to any woman he knew, he'd break his face. And probably a few bones too before having him arrested.

Chapter 11

Apapa, Lagos, Nigeria | November 2019 |

Seun maneuvered her way through the crowd of people and away from the party's noise. It was an interesting party, with a very animated MC, lots of food and several games to make an arcade jealous. The children were having a field day and she had been too, till she started getting overwhelmed.

Plus, her mind had started drifting again, to her pent up sexual frustration.

'Trying to run away I see.'

She jumped with a start and held her hand to her heart. 'You scared me.' She exhaled slowly as Frank walked up to her.

'I'm sorry.' He offered her his elbow and she took it. 'Let's walk.' They walked in silence for a while before Frank broke it. 'I left to get some air too. Been a while since I hosted a party.'

'I understand. It gets pretty overwhelming after a while. And sometimes, we just need air.'

'Exactly.' He turned to her and noticed that she looked worried. It couldn't just be the party making her stressed like this, could it?

'Hug?' He offered. She nodded and let him pull her into a hug. Warning bells rang in her head but she ignored them,

After a few seconds of basking in the simple pleasure of a hug, he pulled back and studied her face again. The look he'd seen in her eyes earlier was back. Fear? Worry? He wasn't sure. And this time, he couldn't let it slide.

'Is there something you want to tell me Seun?'

She looked shocked. She quickly schooled her features but he'd noticed.

'No. Why?'

'You just seem...scared.' He explained.

'Scared? No.' She shook her head and looked right, then down. If only he knew the x-rated thoughts that plagued her mind almost every night.

'I don't believe it.' He lifted her head and looked into her eyes. They were shielded. 'Talk to me. What are you afraid of?'

She rubbed her eyes and shrugged, adjusting her glasses. 'Not being good enough for you.' There. She'd said it out loud. Now she felt like a fool.

'What? What does that even mean?' He shot her a confused look.

'It means what it sounds like.'

'I still don't get it. What are you saying, Seun?'

'I am saying what you heard Frank. Do you want me to spell it out for you?' She let out a heavy breath and flailed her arms around.

'Really?' He was getting angry.

'Yes. See ehn Frank, you're a great guy. You've got a beautiful daughter, a wife that adored you and a good family. You love God, your life is stable and I'm like the exact opposite of that.' Her fears had come out to play. Dozie's words to her had cut way deeper than she realized. The words in Frank's email floated around in her brain.

'Are you listening to yourself Seun?'

'Yes Frank. I can hear myself loud and clear. I have thought about this several times and it never adds up in my head. I drunk-bullied your daughter for God's sake. How can you even love me?' She wanted to stop but she couldn't.

'Seun...' He stared at her in disbelief.

'It's true! I am not good enough.' She shrugged his hands off and began pacing again. 'Think about it.'

'I am not thinking about anything Seun. That is such an absurd thing for you to say. Have I ever said anything like that to you?' He clenched his jaw in barely contained anger.

'You didn't have to. I know. And it's only a matter of time till you realise it too.' She tried to ignore the proximity of their bodies and focus on what she was saying. But concentrating was difficult with him so close.

'Stop this right now Seun. Wherever these ideas came from, dead them.'

'You don't know me. You don't know what I've done. You have no idea who I am. Trust me, you don't want to know the thoughts in my head. If you did, you wouldn't be talking like this.' She looked away.

'I don't care what you've done. All I care about is you, the you that I know now. And I love you. Your past is where it's meant to be and you should leave it there. Whatever you did then doesn't matter as long as you've changed.'

'And what if I haven't?' She challenged him.

'Well, haven't you?' He threw her question back at her.

She didn't answer. Her mind was unsettled and she needed some validation. Desperately.

'Seun.' This whole conversation was going in a way he hadn't planned. He'd hoped to be able to talk to her about his plans for them but she was being irrational. How could she even be thinking like this?

'Seun.' He called her again.

She turned to him and took his hands. Placing them on her waist, she looked up at him and he stared at her in shock. She wrapped her hands behind his neck and pulled him closer, tip-toeing to kiss him. At first he didn't respond and she felt her heart sink.

Told you he doesn't love you.

The thought invaded her head and she started to pull away.

He held her in place, kissing her back with the strength of all his desire and pent-up frustration. Despite their hot exchange just seconds ago, the kiss was a soft, passionate one that had her head spinning round in circles. She felt her heart soar. He did love her. Maybe she'd misjudged him and his feelings towards her.

She kissed his lips, then his cheeks, chin and neck. He moaned slightly and tried to stop her but she wasn't paying attention anymore. She was drowning in her desire for him and need for validation. She felt something in her core shift and everything in her wanted him to make love to her.

'Let's go to my room. It'll only take a few minutes.' She whispered it before she could convince herself not to blurt the words out.

As if a switch had been flipped, he finally summoned the energy to stop. He pulled her hands away from his neck and held her shoulders. 'Seun, this is not right. We should stop right now.'

She looked hurt and it broke his heart. 'You don't want to kiss me? You don't like it?'

'What? No. Of course I want to. I want to kiss you everyday. You have no idea how much.'

'Okay.' She rolled her eyes. 'So what? Are you a virgin?' Her tone was filled with sarcasm.

'Oh come on Seun. Stop doing that.'

'Doing what?'

'Whatever this is.' He ran his hands across his face and looked at her in barely contained frustration.

'Okay. So what's the problem then Frank? You don't want to have sex with me?' She was confused. 'Like, what exactly is wrong?'

'We're losing sight of reason Seun. We need to take it slowly. For one, I do not think we should go to your room.' He grimaced and held her gaze, willing her to understand even as he saw her closing up.

'Why? But you said you love me. And I love you.' Her voice shook and she seemed close to tears.

'Yes I said that and I mean it. I love you. But this isn't love.'

'How is it not? People who love each other show it.'

'You are proposing that we have sex now Seun. Outside of marriage. That's not love, that's lust. I love you and I would like us to do things the right way.'

She wasn't listening. All she could think about was the fact that he was rejecting her. 'So you don't want me?'

'Of course I want you. I want you so bad it hurts. But not now.' She flinched and stepped out of his hold. The pain of his rejection cut deep.

'See. I am not good enough for you and you just proved it Mr. Perfect! You. Don't. Love. Me.'

The bitterness in her voice hurt him. Her words felt like a slap. 'Seun.' His voice was strained with barely contained anger.

'What? You know I'm right Frank. So don't try to deny it.' She shook her head. 'There's someone else right?' That was the only other reason she could think of for why he didn't want her, besides the fact that she was someone else's leftover of course.

Something snapped in him as she spoke and he lost it. 'What is it with you? Didn't you learn anything from your last relationship? Do you always need to be sleeping with someone to feel loved? Are you that desperate?' He knew he should stop but the words kept coming. 'Maybe you are right. You do need to work on yourself!'

'Oh really? Bravo Frank Olumuyiwa. Bravo...' She poked him in the chest and laughed bitterly. 'You know what? I'm done. At least now I know exactly what you think of me.'

As soon as the words left his mouth, he'd regretted them. She was withdrawing from him and he didn't know what to do. 'Look I'm sorry. That came out wrong.' He held her hand as she moved to walk away from him.

She flung his hands away. 'Don't you dare touch me Frank. Stay away from me.'

'Seun.' He called after her.

She didn't look back but her trembling shoulders let him know she was crying.

***

Surulere, Lagos, Nigeria | November 2019 |

He didn't see Seun anymore till the party ended and he didn't want to ask around to avoid any uncomfortable questions. The party ended on a sour note for him and he put up a facade for

Nora so she wouldn't notice anything. She was too perceptive for a seven, well eight year old now.

At home, he couldn't sleep. Thankfully, Kiki had agreed to work the whole day because of the party. She was in Nora's room with her now so he had his room to himself.

To distract himself, he pulled out the book and proceeded to read the last chapter, transfixed...

***

Last entry - December 2019

I'm twenty-two now. My son is five and Dozie, well, he is where he is.

Before you wonder if I'm not scared that he'll ever read this, remember that I know him, like the back of my palm. And I know that he'd rather be caught dead in a park than reading a book. He spends half of his life high on one substance or the other and he most definitely does not know Tabitha the Anon.

I am who I am today because of the empathy of a stranger I met during my mum's nursing home days. Well, she isn't really a stranger anymore, my big mama bear. She volunteered at the nursing home on weekdays and she knew me, because anytime I wasn't with Dozie, I was at my mother's bedside, torn between self-pity, fear, anger and frustration at everyone and everything.

She saw right through my aloof facade and she started to counsel me. For free.

Did I forget to mention that the day my mother died was the day I found out I was pregnant? Haha! It was. A big fat cosmic joke. I felt like the universe was laughing at me.

I ran away from Dozie and I didn't bother going home because there was nothing and no one left for me there. And if I had gone home, Dozie would have found me. Mama took me in and I have never been home since then. It holds the darkest and most miserable memories.

As far as I am concerned, I have no home. My only home is with Mama.

I may not have the next ten years figured out yet. But I have an idea of tomorrow; and of the day after tomorrow.

Yesterday is gone, today is here and tomorrow...well, tomorrow is another day.

And that's enough for me. At least for now.

***

He tossed and turned on his bed till he threw the covers off in frustration. His nerves were on end and instead of distracting him, the book only made him think of Seun more. He felt terrible for how he'd spoken to Seun. Of course, he could argue that he was trying to get them to do the right thing in their relationship but his last words had been too mean and he knew.

'Do you always need to be sleeping with someone to feel loved? Are you that desperate? Maybe you are right. You do need to work on yourself.'

He flinched at the harshness of his own words. No wonder she broke up with him.

But she made me angry too. He struggled within himself.

How could she accuse him of not loving her and of seeing someone else? He was angry too, about how little she thought of herself. Her ex, whoever he was, had broken her more than he realized.

You were wrong. The famous still quiet voice.

Hot tears stung his eyes and he swallowed hard; his throat hurt. He shouldn't have spoken to her that way.

Go to her. The voice again.

'I'll go tomorrow.' He lay down to sleep but he still felt restless. Something was not right and he felt it in his bones.

Go now.

He checked the time. 08:30pm. He woke Kiki up and told her he had to get somewhere urgently.

'What's wrong?' Despite the sleep in her eyes, there was panic in her voice. He couldn't even blame her.

'It's complicated. But just trust me and take care of Nora please.' He fiddled with his keys and tapped his feet. Time was going.

'Okay.' She nodded sleepily. Confusion was still written all over her face. 'Be careful Frank. I'll be praying.'

'Thank you Kiki.' He hurried out and Kiki locked the door behind him.

He got in his car and drove to Temi's Home. All the way there, he tried Seun's number. It was switched off. Temi's line didn't even ring. A strong feeling of looming danger overcame him and he willed the distance to the Home to close faster. The closer he got, the harder he prayed. *God please.*

Chapter 12

Apapa, Lagos, Nigeria | November 2019 |

When she walked away from Frank, she couldn't hold back the tears that poured down her face. She couldn't believe she had broken up with him. Her heart hurt. It seemed every man she'd ever loved thought so low of her. He'd called her desperate.

Desperate. The word tasted like a bitter pill on her tongue. More tears poured.

She entered her apartment and settled on the bed. Uzi was with Temi and would probably spend the night with her. The apartment felt eerily quiet and she heard the sounds from the party in the distance. Stripping her clothes, she ran a warm bath and let her tears mix with the water.

There was a rock where her heart should have been. Frank had rejected her.

I told you he doesn't love you. But no, you didn't listen to me.

Biting down on her lips till it hurt, she stepped out of the bath and slipped into a night dress, ready to call it an early night even though it was just evening. All she wanted was to curl up in bed and sleep away her sorrows. Tomorrow, she'd think about her life.

Going to bed, she drifted off into a fitful sleep. When she opened her eyes again, it was dark outside and there was no light. Her eyes flew to Uzi's bed in the corner and panic filled her till she remembered that he was with Temi. Turning on her phone torchlight, she headed to the kitchen to get some water and crackers. By the time she was done eating, there was light again and she made her way back to the room, lost in thought.

Letting her mind drift to Frank's kiss, she closed her eyes and reminisced.

I want to kiss you everyday. I want you so bad it hurts.

A smile creeped across her face and she paused in the hallway, playing back the memory.

But not now.

The smile quickly disappeared. Right. He'd rejected her. She grit her teeth and kept walking towards the room.

As she got into her room, the hairs on her arms and neck stood and she looked around quickly. It seemed like someone else was in the house with her. She froze in her tracks and her ears perked up as the sounds of someone moving around floated to her. Someone else was definitely in the house. She'd forgotten to lock the door in her hurry earlier.

Temi's Home was pretty safe and there was security all round so she shouldn't be so afraid. But if the person in her house had good intentions, he or she would have knocked like a normal person instead of walking in just because the door had been left open. Something fishy was going on.

She reached for her phone to call for help and realised that she'd left it in the kitchen. Whispering a silent prayer, she grabbed on to the nearest thing she saw that could serve as a weapon: a red heeled shoe at the foot of her bed. Slowly and as quietly as possible, she tiptoed to the back of the room door and waited, grateful that at least, Uzi wasn't in harm's way with her. More than ever, she regretted not replacing her room's lock. It was broken.

Soon enough, the footstep sounds stopped right in front of her room door. She bit her tongue and held her breath.

The door opened.

She swung her hand up, ready to attack.

But it fell limply to her side when she saw who it was. The shoe slipped out of her grip and to the ground.

'Hi princess.' He smiled and winked at her. The silver earring on his left ear glinted in the dimly lit room.

'Dozie.' His name left her lips as no more than a whisper. It was all she could muster. She should scream but her vocal cords were barely connecting with her brain.

'Miss me?' He stepped closer to her. The faint smell of weed on his breath drifted to her nostrils and she felt heady.

'Uh-' She could only stutter. Goosebumps rose all over her arms but beneath her contempt for him, she felt a familiar stirring in her core.

He took another step towards her and their eyes locked.

You aren't worth anything. You are my leftover.

She blinked and licked her lips. Her mouth suddenly felt so dry. The first instinct she had was to step back. Yet she stood, rooted to the spot.

Maybe he was right. She was his leftover.

Her eyes dropped to his lips and she saw them curve into a smile.

'Aww. You want me already.' He stretched out a hand to cup her left cheeks and she closed her eyes, leaning into his touch. Tears stung her eyes but she swallowed them down.

At least someone wanted her.

He pinned her to the wall and she whimpered. In a split second, he'd closed the small gap between them. Leaning forward, he covered her lips in his and kissed her. His kisses were never gentle or sweet. Always urgent and unrelenting.

She rested her flat palms on his chest and kissed him back, throwing caution to the wind. Her brain told her to push him away but she wasn't thinking straight. Within a few seconds, they were out of breath and panting in between kisses.

'You're mine, you know that right?' He said gruffly.

She nodded helplessly. Her knees felt like jelly and she leaned on to him for support.

Frank. His face invaded her thoughts and she froze.

'What?' Dozie whispered in her ears as he nibbled her ears.

'Nothing.' She lied.

'Hm.' He was distracted. His hands slipped under her dress and groped. 'I want to hear you say it.'

'Say what?' Moaning slightly, she leaned closer into him.

'My name.' He muttered, still nibbling and groping.

'Dozie.' Hearing his name from her own lips felt like cold water pouring down her body and as his hands moved lower to her thighs, it hit her. This was Dozie, her ex and nemesis. She should be screaming her lungs out and pushing him away, not about to fall into bed with him again. She froze for the second time.

His hands stopped moving and this time, he looked at her with steely, cold eyes.

In one swift motion, she slipped out of his hold and hurried out the door. He followed her and caught up quickly. Spinning her around, he lifted her to the hallway table and stood in between her legs.

'Playing games I see.' The smile on his face was barely masking his anger. He squinted his eyes at her, daring her to disagree. She couldn't say she was running away from him. He had her pinned down and if she screamed now, he'd hit her. Holding her breath, she looked at him and nodded. Her whole body was trembling.

Rubbing her arms up and down, his gaze softened a bit and he leaned closer to her, resting his forehead on hers.

'Are you cold? You've got goosebumps.'

'Y-yes, I mean, no. No, I'm not c-c-cold.' She stuttered.

'Don't be scared. I won't hurt you.' He murmured. 'I love you.' He kissed her neck.

Love? What did he know about love?

She shivered, more out of fear than anything else. Her eyes slipped shut and she sent up a silent prayer. Mustering all her energy, she positioned her knee to kick him in the guts and run.

The door opening had them both looking up. Frank stood in the doorway, eyes wide and shocked. He shot her an accusatory look before his eyes locked with Dozie's.

Oh crap.

She looked from one man to the other as they faced each other off silently. Dozie had a smug smile on his face while Frank's eyebrows twitched. The skin around Frank's jaw was stretched thin as he gritted his teeth. Breaking the stare, he turned around and slammed the door behind him.

'Wait!' Seun pulled away from the embrace and straightened her clothes. She rushed out after Frank, ignoring Dozie's warnings. Frank was already out the door and her steps quickened into a jog as she tried to catch up with him on shaky legs.

'What have I done?'

'Frank wait!' she shouted again. He didn't stop and the growing feeling of panic in her throat threatened to choke her. She could feel him slipping away from her and there didn't seem to be anything she could do about it. She had betrayed him and now she was going to lose him.

'Seun, come back here!' Dozie's menacing voice echoed through the hallway and she ran faster. She knew that tone. Trouble was brewing.

Chills went through her bones as she heard him catching up behind her.

'Seun!' His voice boomed.

She heaved heavily and willed her legs to move faster.

How on earth had she ever fallen in love with someone so inhuman? And worse still, why on earth did she keep letting him into her life?

'How dare you?' His fist rammed into her neck before she heard his voice. She slumped forward as a scream escaped her lips. Pulling her back by the hair, he slapped her hard across the face and threw her against the wall.

'Let go of me Dozie!' She cried and scratched at thin air. Blood was gushing from her nose and cheeks and she couldn't see clearly anymore. Her left arm felt numb.

This is the man you were just about to tumble into bed with stupid. This is who you chose over Frank? Her subconscious taunted her even as she fell to the ground.

Dozie lifted his hand to land another blow and she squeezed her eyes shut, bracing herself for the impact. It never came. Instead, she heard a loud grunt.

Shocked, she opened her eyes just in time to see Frank's fist collide with Dozie's nose. He crashed into the side table.

Krrrr. She didn't know if it was Dozie's nose or Frank's knuckles but something had definitely broken. Maybe both.

Frank landed several punches on Dozie's body and didn't stop till Seun's whimpering in the corner brought him back to reality.

Landing one last kick, he hurried to Seun's side and carried her. She felt limp in his hands and looking at her broke his heart.

'I'm sorry.' She whispered, a second before her world went black.

***

Lifemate Private Hospital, Ikeja, Lagos, Nigeria | November 2019 |

Temi went to a nearby restaurant to buy some food and Frank stood alone in the hospital room, watching Seun sleep. He felt everything from anger to hurt, shame and regret. But one thing was certain, he loved this woman with every fibre of his being. He hadn't meant to knock the man unconscious, just incapacitate him. But seeing him hit Seun like that had him seeing red.

Dozie had ended up with 2 cracked ribs, a broken nose and several other minor injuries. He was sure it would have been worse if he hadn't stopped when he did. And it served the man right for daring to lay his hands on Seun. The police were handling his case now but if it was up to him alone, he'd make sure the man served jail term for a long time.

The image of the two of them kissing floated into his head again and he couldn't get rid of it. He knew his words had been too harsh earlier but he didn't imagine in a million years that she would go back to her ex.

He was still in shock from discovering that Seun's ex and her son's father was named Dozie. Something in his head told him that this Dozie wasn't different from the one he read about in the book he'd borrowed from Christian. And if he was putting two and two together correctly, Seun was Tabitha the Anon. The thought had his brain spinning. Was that why she was always so secretive and closed off?

Images of Dozie throwing Seun against the wall filled his mind next and he swallowed down the urge to cry.

This was the woman he wanted to marry for heaven's sake. The person who'd be his mother's daughter. His heart sank. What was the appeal this guy held for her? He was hurting; for her and for himself. But more for her.

He wanted to break something. As he looked down at his bandaged knuckles, something in him snapped and he shook his head. He needed some space to think. And he needed it soon.

'Frank, you've been here all night and it's almost noon. At least get something to eat.' Temi urged him when she got back.

'Ah ma, I was actually just leaving.' He consoled himself with the thought that Karen would be able to keep an eye on Seun till she got well. Perks of having family at your hospital.

Even though he tried to hide it, Temi caught the look in his eyes. She could sense him battling within himself; caught between his love for Seun and the reality of her cheating on him.

'Okay my son. Take care.'

He squared his shoulders as he walked out of the room and Temi wondered if he was walking out of Seun's life for good.

'God please help your children. Please.'

Temi looked heavenward and murmured a prayer.

'God please help your children. Please.'

She repeated the prayer and let her shoulders slump for a second. Fatigue washed over her, reminding her of how tired she was, of being everyone's hero and of missing her late husband.

***

Seun woke up with a banging headache. She still felt groggy from the sedatives and it took only a second for all the events from yesterday to unfold in her head. She tried to facepalm but let her hand fall back to the bed as a sharp pain ran through it. Turning on her side, she searched the room for Frank hoping that what she feared hadn't happened. She was met with Temi's probing eyes.

'Frank.' Her voice was little more than a whisper.

Temi pursed her lips and shook her head from side to side. Her face said it all. 'He's gone.'

'Hm.' Seun's face creased into a grimace and she fell back against the bed.

'And I don't think he's coming back.'

'Frank.' Seun kept muttering his name as she broke down into tears. Temi wrapped her in a hug and she melted into it, biting down on her tongue to keep from groaning. Pain soared through her body but she wanted so much to remain in the hug and bask in the temporary peace it afforded her. When she could no longer take it, she eased out of the hug and turned towards the wall. Her heart was breaking into a million pieces.

'I'm sorry.' Temi murmured and looked on into space. Her heart was heavy.

Seun buried her face in the pillow and cried. All she could think about was getting discharged and going to beg for his forgiveness. She'd crawl and snivel at his feet if she had to. And she held on to a tiny sliver of hope that he hadn't finished reading her book and couldn't put the puzzle pieces together. Because if he had, then she was truly screwed.

I have been such a fool.

Chapter 13

Surulere, Lagos, Nigeria | November 2019 |

Seun walked towards Frank's apartment and a strong feeling of dejavu came over her. It felt like history was repeating itself as she got closer to the door. Her mind flashed back to the day she'd gone back to Temi's Home. That day, she'd been scared to call. But in this case, she'd been calling him for days since she got discharged. To no avail.

He wasn't picking her calls and she always let it ring till it couldn't anymore, hoping each time that he'd pick up. She could hum his caller tune in her sleep and if she counted all her fingers and toes, they still wouldn't be enough for all the texts she'd sent him.

It registered in her brain that his car was in the parking lot so he was most likely around. Her palms got sweaty and she placed her hand over her chest, willing her heart to stop beating so fast. Frank hadn't been coming to work and she knew that he wasn't with Christian because she had called to ask.

'I haven't seen him in days Seun. What's up?' Christian sounded concerned and she wished she hadn't called to get him worried.

'Oh nothing. I'm just a little bothered because his number hasn't been going.'

'Ah yes I remember. I think he mentioned something about going to Akure for a weekend but we haven't spoken since then so I don't know if he's left. Didn't he tell you?'

'Um yeah, I think he mentioned it. Haha, it must have skipped my mind. Thank you Christian. I'll call him later. I'm sure everything is fine. It's probably a network problem.' She lied through her teeth.

'Alright dear. Hope you're recovering well?'

'Yes thank you.' She involuntarily flexed her left arm and winced a little. It still hurt.

'Take care of you okay.'

She climbed up the stairs and murmured a small prayer. Taking a deep breath and holding it, she knocked on the door.

Nothing.

She knocked some more.

Still nothing.

'Frank, I know you're in there. Open the door please. I'm sorry.' She shuffled from one foot to the other and waited.

Nothing.

'Babe, I promise I didn't mean to. It'll never happen again please.' Her voice echoed back at her through the corridor. She didn't even care if Nora was in there with him, hearing everything she was saying. It didn't bother her as neighbours walked past and stared at her like a crazy person. Even she felt like a crazy person. She was going crazy waiting to hear from him.

'Please Frank, let's talk about it. I've been calling and texting. I beg you please, stop ignoring me. I don't know what else to do.' She kept baring her heart. When she didn't get a response, she tried the doorbell, knowing fully well that it was broken. The longer she waited, the more helpless she felt. Why wasn't he coming to the door?

She called him again, hoping that he'd pick this time. A tiny voice in her head told her he obviously wouldn't and sadly, it was right. After knocking and ringing the broken bell several times, she rested her back on the door and sank to the ground. Burying her face in her palms, she burst into tears.

'Please.' She whispered through her tears.

After several long minutes that felt like hours, her cries reduced to mere whimpers and she sat there, tapping limply at the door. Maybe he now hated her too much to care.

***

Frank had just dropped Nora off at Taiwo's house. He was taking a break and going to Akure to clear his head. He'd barely been gone for thirty minutes when Christian's call came in.

'Bro, what's up now? You didn't tell Seun you were going out of town.' Christian crooned through the receiver.

It took everything in him not to slam the steering wheel in frustration. It was a rented car and he didn't want to add payment for damages to his problems at the moment.

He hadn't told Christian a thing and he'd also been banking on the fact that she wouldn't call him to avoid raising suspicion. That was exactly why he'd dropped Nora with Taiwo and Karen instead of with Christian.

Apparently, she'd wanted to see him badly enough to take a chance. It made him smile a little but the smile quickly disappeared as he remembered what she had done again.

Thinking quickly, he tried to deflect the question with a question of his own.

'She told you that?'

'No she didn't. She told me some gibberish about forgetting that you told her. But I know her and I know you. She blabs when she's uncomfortable or trying to lie. She was definitely lying. And you my brother, are deflecting.'

So much for avoiding the question.

'Did you guys have a fight?'

'No.' He paused as an angry driver honked at him for moving too slowly. 'I mean yes. Sort of. It's complicated.'

'Really?'

'Yes.' He scratched his beard and pulled up by the roadside. He couldn't concentrate on driving and the incessant horning was getting unbearable..

'Well, whatever it is, you should call her. She sounded worried sick.' Christian paused and took a deep breath. He wanted to say more but it was none of his business. And he didn't think they'd appreciate his meddling. He settled for a simple advice. 'Take care bro and don't do anything stupid.'

Frank hung up and let his head drop to the steering. The horn blared loudly and he jumped back with a start, hissing through his teeth.

At this point, whoever invented horns was not in his good books.

His eyes burned with tears. How on earth had he thought he could make this trip to Akure in this state? He was a mess.

'She sounded worried sick'. Christian's voice played in his head and he dismissed the guilt that pulled at his heart. She was the one that caused this and he wanted so much to hold on to his anger. As usual, his desire to hold and hug her started to take over. And as usual, he pushed it to the back of his mind. He wasn't ready to go there just yet.

He sighed in frustration and drove into a nearby building parking lot. He'd call the rental company to get it later. Ordering a taxi, he made the trip back home, lost in thought.

***

Frank walked up the stairs to his apartment. He stopped dead in his tracks when he saw Seun. She was sitting cross-legged, hunched-shoulders and head-in-palms in front of his door. From the way her body shook and her soft whimpers, he knew she was crying. Exhaling, he rubbed his face down with a handkerchief and fought the urge to rush to her and wrap his arms around her.

She looked up then and their eyes locked. They stared at each other for seemingly endless seconds. Tears dropped down her cheeks and Frank's face was a mask of pain. The both of them were mentally and physically exhausted.

'Frank.' She croaked his name and scrambled to her feet. Hurrying towards him, she held his hands and rushed out, 'I'm sorry. What you saw, it's not what you think...' Her voice trailed off.

He avoided looking at her, instead, focusing on his stiff hands in hers.

'It's not what you think.' The famous cheat line.

They were both thinking the same thing. Could their relationship survive this rough patch?

Frank's lips stretched into a thin line and he handed her his handkerchief before pulling his hands away; watching her clean her eyes from the side of his eyes. The sight of her crying at his doorstep hurt his heart and again, all he wanted to do was hug her, tell her everything would be okay. But he didn't. Instead, he walked towards his apartment door with determined strides, fighting the urge to look back.

Following him closely behind, she held his hand again and turned him to face her. He raised an eyebrow in question and froze when she went on her knees.

'Please Frank. Just hear me out. Give me a chance to explain.' Seun begged. Her tone was tinged with desperation and fear.

Something in him snapped and he lashed out at her. 'Explain what Seun? You want to explain to me about how we had one fight and you fell back into your ex's arms.' He paused and shook his head. 'Or wait, maybe you'd like to explain to me how on God's earth you mistakenly started making out with him at almost midnight, in your apartment. How about we start there Seun?' His words came out in clipped tones and they hurt. Terribly.

More tears stung her eyes and she wiped them off frantically. Now was not the time. Now she was fighting for another chance with the man she loved. Now she needed her head, not her mushy heart making her cry and fumble.

'It's not like that.' Her voice came out shaky.

'Then tell me Seun, how is it? How. Is. It?' He pinned her with bored eyes and she wilted under the heat of his gaze.

In that moment she wished the ground would open up to swallow her. She hadn't thought of what she would say when she got here. All that had been on her mind was to see him and beg for his forgiveness. And now, her tongue felt tied. 'I-I-I...' she stuttered.

'I thought so.' He spat out the words, before shaking her hands off a second time and heading for his door.

Seeing his back turned to her felt so final and from somewhere deep within her, she somehow found her tongue. She struggled to her feet and stumbled over her words. 'I didn't plan it. It just happened I promise you.'

'Hm, but you didn't push him away did you? For all I know, you were probably even waiting for him to come, knowing he would. Tell me Seun, was that even the first time?' He turned to face her again and this time she saw the eyebags under his eyes. Just like her, he hadn't been sleeping. The thought warmed her heart a little; at least he was affected too.

'It's...complicated.' She said, letting her hands fall to her sides limply.

'Really? That's the best you can come up with? It's complicated?' He let out a mirthless laugh. 'Is that why you didn't tell me about Dozie? About the book? Your family?' His impassive mask had fallen. All she could see on his face was pure anguish, his voice dripped with the pain of betrayal and her shoulders grew heavy with the weight of guilt. He'd pieced the puzzle together.

An almost inaudible whisper of 'I'm sorry.' was all she could manage and Frank stared at her incredulously.

'Sorry?' He ground his teeth and snorted. 'Sorry.' He repeated. Seun nodded helplessly.

'We were in a relationship, Seun. I allowed you into my life. My daughter's life! Jesus! Your son literally adores me right now. I could actually see a future with us. And you didn't think for once in the last few months to mention something, anything at all, to me?'

'I thought about it. And I was going to but...' Her voice cracked. There was no defense that would make sense now.

'But you didn't.' He finished for her.

'I wasn't sure about the relationship Frank.' She blurted the truth, staring down at her feet.

'There you go again, confusing me. First you say you're not good enough for me and that I don't love you. Where those ideas came from, I can't understand for the life of me. Now it's 'not being sure' of our relationship? At every turn Seun, I constantly reassured you. Every turn. And if after all that, you still didn't believe, what exactly did you want from me?' He had one hand on his hips and the other on his forehead, massaging.

'Look, we are not children Seun. You may have youth on your side but we can both agree that we've each had an unfair share of 'life's bitter lemons'. And I don't know about you Seun but I do not have time for games. I don't.'

She grimaced. 'You say you love me but you don't show it.'

'And by show you mean, kissing you senseless and jumping into bed with you? I am not that type of man Seun. I love you. And trust me, I love your body too. But I know what I want. And I know what God's word says.' He paused briefly, fighting hard to school his features. 'For heaven's sake Seun, you know what I mean. I know you do. So why are you making this more difficult?'

Seun squeezed her eyes shut and let his words sink in. Many christians had sex outside marriage. The bible was an archaic book. Why on earth did he feel so strongly about this? She thought.

'I read the book Seun. Every single page from cover to cover like you asked us to. I know what happened to you and I am truly sorry. But this is not how life should be. This is not the type of life I want. And you shouldn't want it either. It is not the right way. Don't you get it?'

She nodded slowly. 'But, not everyone is toxic like Dozie.' She bit her lips. 'I know many people who had sex outside marriage and still have good relationships and marriages. And I know people who waited and still had crappy marriages, with or without children in the equation.' Reaching out to touch his face, she trailed her finger along his lips and leaned up to kiss him. He turned his face so the kiss landed on his cheeks instead.

When he looked back, he saw the hurt in her eyes. Their eyes locked and an electric tension passed between them. Seun's lips were slightly parted and Frank felt like they were literally begging to be kissed again.

Licking his parched lips, he gauged the situation in his head. His door was right behind him and Nora wasn't home. They could easily go in and do anything they wanted. Yet even as he thought it, he knew he wouldn't do that.

He couldn't.

Yes, Seun was more than willing and Lord knew he was more than a little turned on. But he didn't want to take advantage of her. She was so deeply hurt and he could finally read that her trauma made her definition of love quite thwarted. Whatever experience she'd had with rehab and her therapist, it wasn't nearly sufficient for the healing she needed.

A thought suddenly popped in his head.

'Did you get my letter Seun? Or should I say, Tabitha?'

Her eyes widened and her hands flew to her lips. She thought of lying for a second and then banished the thought. No point hiding again at this stage. The cat was already out of the bag. 'Yes.'

Taking a deep breath, he said the words that felt like lead in his mouth. 'I think we should give each other some space.'

'What?' Confused and cross, she gaped at him.

'I mean it Seun. Our beliefs are not aligned and, you're still in love with your ex.'

'Frank, I am not in love with Dozie. It's you I love.' Her eyes were pinned on the ground like it was the most interesting artwork in the world.

'I find that ironic. He's behind bars right now, yet I still feel like I'm fighting him for your love. Really, I wish this was all just a big bad dream but it's not. It's real. And it hurts.' He rubbed his neck slightly before lifting her head so that her eyes were level with his. 'Tell me Seun. Was that the only time you went back to him?' He wanted so much to forgive her but tiny pins of jealousy were jumping around in his stomach.

'No.' She nodded. 'I-I-mean, yes.' She shook her head.

Frank squinted at her and raised an eyebrow. 'I see.'

'Like I said, it's complicated. Once, before I met you, we got together. And that was the only time, I promise you. After then, I knew it was so wrong and I went back to Temi immediately. That was the day we met at the home. We got a court injunction then, ordering him to stay away from us or face the consequences. He's stayed away so far. Well, at least until you-know-when.'

'Hm. And by 'got together' you mean?'

'Sex.' She replied flatly.

'Right.' The word lodged in his brain and stayed there.

'That was the only time. What you saw that day, I had just woken up for a night snack and was going back to bed to wonder why I was so undesirable to you...'

He cut her off. 'You're not undesirable to me...'

'Let me finish!'

'Okay, okay.' He raised both hands in surrender.

'And then, I heard movement in the house. It was him. He came on to me Frank. I was hurt, tired a-and horny. We had history and you had rejected me.' She bit her lip.

'So now it's my fault?' He felt like someone was now hammering pins into his stomach walls.

'No. It's just...' Her voice trailed off. 'Look, I didn't plan to. My head told me not to but my body had other plans. Once what I was doing and who I was doing it with clicked, I wanted to push him away and run so bad. I know how d-dangerous he can get.'

'Wow Sherlock, you don't say?' He rolled his eyes.

She swallowed. 'And then you walked in.'

'Hm.' He looked at her for a long moment. Her narration was hard to believe but she looked sincere enough.

'Look, it's been a long day Seun. I'm tired and I don't think I have the emotional strength for this right now. And like I said before, I think we should take a break.'

'Okay.' She wiped the lone tear that ran down her cheeks. He wasn't going to take her back.

'I didn't see your car outside.'

'I came in a taxi. Can't exactly be driving myself just yet. I know you don't care about me but there are other drivers on the road you know. Driving in this state is a death trap waiting to happen.' She looked up at him sadly.

'You think I don't care?' He folded his arms and pinned her with a look.

'Oh God Frank. Spare me the sympathy please. I'm leaving. So you don't have to worry about me draining your strength any-more.'

'You know it's not like that.'

'Oh but it is exactly like that.' A lone tear rolled down her cheek and she wiped it off angrily.

He didn't answer and she nodded, a sad smile plastered on her face. 'And, that's my cue.' She turned to leave.

'Come on, I'll order you a taxi.' He held her arm to lead her down the stairs but she shrugged it off.

'I can manage on my own thank you.' She replied coolly.

He looked at her. Like, really looked at her. There were still signs of bruises on her body. 'Are you okay Seun?' He touched the bruise on her arm.

Again, she shrugged him off.

'I'm fine.'

'You sure?' This time, he traced the harsh scar on her neck and she flinched.

'I said I'm fine!' She screamed at him, whirling around and hurrying towards the stairs.

He followed her and grabbed her hands, pulling her towards him in one swift motion.

She gasped and stared at him with daggers in her eyes. She was livid.

Ignoring her glare, he did what he had wanted to do since he saw. He pulled her into a hug.

At first she struggled and pounded against his chest, crying. But he didn't let go and she eventually crumpled into his arms, allowing him to hold her. He let her cry into his chest, smoothing her hair slowly before dropping a light kiss on her forehead. 'I'm sorry.'

'No Frank. I'm sorry. You can't even begin to imagine how much.'

In the end, they both agreed that a break might do them some good even though the uncertainty of their future together hung thick in the air like a fog. He ordered a taxi for her and walked her to the car.

'So this is it I guess?' She asked, more unshed tears swimming in her eyes.

He shook his head.

'Don't bother about answering that.' Settling into the back seat, she looked straight ahead. The car zoomed off and Frank stood there, staring at it till it disappeared. She didn't look back once.

Watching her go, he felt a deep sense of loss that he didn't dare to acknowledge till he was safely behind his apartment door. Away from her pleading eyes and sad smile, he sank to the ground. And cried.

Chapter 14

Yaba, Lagos, Nigeria | December 2019 |

It was Christmas season and Seun needed to find a church to attend service. She didn't want to go to the Home's chapel and for some reason, going to Temi's regular church didn't appeal to her. So she went on Instagram and searched for one. The first church that popped up was Anthem of Hope International. She copied the address down and typed it into Google Maps.

Sure, she could have easily stayed home today. But she didn't want to be alone with her thoughts on Christmas day. Thankfully, Dozie was out of the picture. She'd gone back to therapy and her walk with God had really blossomed since her painful break up with Frank. He insisted on calling it a break but it didn't feel like one to her. It felt like a break up.

And for this day, there was a nudge in her spirit to attend the Anthem of Hope service. She'd been seeing flyers online for months now, and today was as good a time as any.

With Uzi's seatbelt securely done, she headed to the church in Yaba, conservatively dressed in a white shirt and plain jeans.

Pulling Uzi along, she sat in the back pew and paid attention. From the corner of her eye, she saw Mrs. Dede take the pulpit to lead praise and worship and her jaw dropped. Mrs Dede was a worship leader? The woman had never struck her as a religious person. But then again, she didn't really know her.

Seun tried to pay attention through the service but curiosity ate at her the whole time. But one passage the Pastor mentioned stuck with her despite being extremely distracted.

'The LORD is close to the brokenhearted; he saves those whose spirits are crushed.' - □□*Psalms*□ □*34:18*□

This is so for me, she thought, wondering for the umpteenth time if she'd lost Frank forever, before resuming stalking Mrs Dede with her eyes. Trailing Mrs Dede's movements across the room, their eyes finally locked. She looked away quickly but it was too late. The woman had seen her. And she was smiling and waving! Seun smiled sheepishly and waved back hoping to slip away unnoticed before the service ended,

'Hi there.' Seun almost jumped out of her skin when she turned and saw Mrs Dede standing behind her.

'H-hello ma. Good evening.' She stretched out her trembling fingers for a handshake and Mrs Dede only stared at it for a brief second.

'Oh come on drop the formalities Seun. And lose the 'ma'. Call me Anna.' Moving in for a hug, she caught Seun off-guard. For a split second, Seun froze in her arms before she relaxed. Anna smelled really nice.

'Okay A-aunty Anna.' She hugged her back, wondering about the appropriateness of calling her editor by her first name.

'Aunty. Hm.' Anna muttered the word as if she was trying to determine if she liked the taste of it. It didn't seem to Seun like she did. 'Fair enough.' She finally said.

Seun shot her a clipped smile. It was the best she could muster considering the awkwardness of the situation.

'First time here?' Anna asked her, pulling back. She pulled her jet straight weave behind one ear and smiled winningly.

Seun licked her dry lips, trying hard not to stare at Anna's legs. Her heels were ankle-breaking. As usual. 'Yes.'

'Well, you might want to consider staying. It's an amazing family.' She smiled widely and it unnerved Seun. This woman that knew everything about her yet always seemed so non judgemental. She didn't think anyone but Temi could be like that.

'Did you enjoy the service?'

'Yes I did ma. I mean, Anna. A-aunty. Anna.'

How much worse could this possibly get?

Seun still observed her with suspicion. Most of the christians she knew were highly judgemental and hypocritical, and many of them regarded her with thinly veiled disdain. It gave her a good excuse to avoid The Church as much as she could. Being a single mum wasn't exactly church poster card material either.

'Great. Well, I'm the head chorister here. If you need any help, just let me know dear. I hope you stick around Seun.'

If only she knew this was a one-off thing. *Why would I come back here?* She thought.

'Bye for now.' Another smile. Another hug. And then she was gone, leaving Seun reeling in mild shock. What were the odds that she'd pick a random church from off Instagram and end up in her editor's church?

Bye for now. She'd said it like she was sure Seun would come back and maybe she had been sure. Because despite her initial plan to not go back to the church, she found herself going there several times for other programmes, including crossover service. And as hard as she'd tried not to be, she'd been drawn into the church, the love that oozed from everyone there and Mrs Dede, well Aunty Anna's surprisingly caring nature that she'd somehow missed in the past.

She actually loved it at Anthem of Hope and she spent more and more time there into the new year. She discovered more about herself and the grace of God. And she wanted so much to take Frank up on the call he'd offered in his letter to Tabitha.

But he'd been quite clear in their last conversation. 'I think we should take a break.' Really? That was as good a break up as anyone else. Maybe even worse. It sounded like a thinly veiled attempt to not say what he really meant. He didn't want her.

Knowing that if she thought about it for too long, she'd burst into tears as per usual, she opened her bible and read, learning, distracting herself and whiling away time.

***

Surulere, Lagos, Nigeria | January 2020 |

He looked up and saw Seun riding a bicycle in the distance. As he got closer, something shocking struck him. She was riding in circles and not only was she riding in circles, she was riding around a large, black, endless pit.

All the hair on his skin stood and his heart jumped into his mouth, then back down. 'Seun!' He screamed her name multiple times but it was like she couldn't hear him. He ran towards her, desperately screaming for her to move away from the pit.

She looked up and stared straight at him but it felt like she was looking right through him. Then it hit him. She couldn't see him. But it appeared she could hear him, because she kept staring. Then, she looked away.

With every second that passed, her bike wobbled and she got too close to the edge.

'Pay attention to where you're riding. Move away from the edge.' He screamed, beads of sweat making trails down his face and across his entire body.

She looked up again, like the voice had cut through her thoughts. Still seeing nothing, she turned back to the bike and looked ahead. The pit was right in front of her now.

'No!' Frank screamed, as her bike tipped over the edge. He opened his mouth to scream again and then....

He woke up.

Sweating profusely, he threw off the blanket and removed his damp shirt. He tried to regulate his heavy breathing and ended up doubling over in a coughing fit that had him wheezing. Soon the coughing turned to slow gaps and he looked down to find his hands shaking. His whole body was trembling as wracking sobs escaped his lips.

What is this Lord?

He didn't know what to do. The dream had felt so real.

Pray.

He prayed and wept profusely. He prayed for the child that Seun had been, the woman she was and that her pain would ease. Although he had been the one to ask for a break, he found himself changing his mind. Seun needed him.

No. She needs me.

The reality hit him like a pack of cards and his shoulders slumped. He felt deflated and helpless.

Pray.

He spent the rest of the night praying Psalm 118:17 over Seun. 'You won't die, you will live and declare what the LORD has done...'

He prayed till he drifted off into a fitful sleep.

***

Staring at his phone for the hundredth time that morning, Frank willed himself to focus on his work. He'd taken time off volunteering but he was spending his time setting up investments in fintech and surveying property to buy. His phone screen displayed his contact list.

He'd searched for Seun's name, holding himself back from calling her every time he wanted to press the green button. His hands itched to call her, talk to her, touch her, hug her pain away, confirm that she was okay. Clenching them into fists, he looked at his laptop screen again, trying his hardest to pay attention to the investment he was about to make.

Two seconds later, the phone screen flashed and his ringtone permeated the air. It was Seun. Panic filled him and he stared at the phone, transfixed, unable to pick it. What would he say? The dream was still so fresh in his subconscious. It rang again and stopped. Then kept ringing till he couldn't ignore it anymore.

'Hello.' He finally picked the call.

Seun's frantic voice floated through the receiver and a lump lodged itself in his throat.

'Frank...' Her voice cracked and he could barely hear her over her sobs.

Something was definitely wrong. Remembering the dream again, dread filled him. He sat up and put the phone on speaker. 'Seun, what is it? Calm down and talk to me. Is something wrong with Uzi, Temi...you?'

'T-Temi, Temi is...Temi...'

'What? Talk to me baby. What happened to Temi?' He felt his blood run cold.

'Temi is...' She sighed heavily into the receiver and launched into another bout of tears.

'What? What happened to Temi?' He asked softly. Even as he asked, he feared for the answer she would give. Was the woman sick?

'Temi is dead, Frank.'

'What? How?' His head was spinning. He'd been expecting bad news but this...this was shattering.

'We w-were going somewhere together but I s-s-suddenly had a runny stomach so she left without me.' She paused to sniff and Frank could almost swear he heard the sound of his own heart pounding in his chest. 'Sh-she had a heart attack while driving her c-car and got in an accid-dent...' She kept crying and he froze in time, staring at his phone as if it had suddenly grown horns.

'Frank? Are you there?'

'Yes. Seun, where are you?' He stood up and picked his car keys, heading for the door. He was torn between relief that Seun was fine and anguish that Temi was everything but.

'I'm at the hospital. We're all here.' Seun replied through her tears.

'I am on my way okay. Just stay put.'

'Okay.'

Changing his mind at the last minute, he dropped his keys, too disoriented to drive. Instead, he ordered a taxi, and headed straight to the hospital.

Chapter 15

Lifemate Private Hospital, Ikeja, Lagos, Nigeria | January 2020 |

Seun paced back and forth in the hospital waiting area, clenching and unclenching her fist. Silent tears rolled down her eyes.

Karen and Taiwo sat in a corner, silently praying. Karen, in her blue hospital scrubs and Taiwo, in work clothes. Anita, Temi's other daughter, was speaking with the doctor about moving the body to the morgue. And Tosan, stood alone by the room, staring into space. Everyone was overcome in their own grief.

Searching for a free chair, Seun plopped into it and pulled her legs up, hugging her knees to her chin. She wanted to shrink smaller and smaller till she disappeared. Her brain told her to wait for someone who'd come to pinch her awake from this nightmare. Or tell her they'd made a mistake and Temi was in fact, very much alive.

No one came. And she let her tears flow freely.

She couldn't believe that just a week ago, she'd been discussing the TV interview with Temi. She'd told Aunty Anna she felt she might be ready and Temi had encouraged her. As always.

'It's your call baby. And remember, no pressure. Do it only because you want to, and if you feel God leading you. No matter what people say, only what God says about you matters.' And then she'd hugged her and walked out of her apartment, leaving her to chew on the words.

That was just one week ago. A week ago, she would have never imagined that this would happen. Not in a million years.

She'd called Frank, because he was the first person that occurred to her to call. She couldn't call Dozie or any of her old friends and she didn't have any family close enough to matter. She had no idea what she'd say to him when he got here. But maybe they'd need no words. He'd said he was coming hadn't he? Right now, that was all she needed. Him. To cheer her up, and tell her everything would be fine even though he couldn't be sure.

And his hugs. Oh, how she missed his hugs. It'd been too long.

A movement at the entrance drew her attention and she looked up to see Frank. Without missing a beat, she rushed into his arms and wrapped her hands around his chest. She hugged him tight like her life depended on it and he didn't complain, even though she was cutting off his oxygen supply.

He hugged her back, rubbing her hair to soothe her, like a child. He felt so protective of her and inwardly, he wondered what he'd have done if it had been Seun in that accident. God forbid.

If he remembered anything about the last time they'd seen, he didn't show it. And despite the guilt that once again, gnawed at her insides, she was just grateful for his presence.

He quietly led her to a seat before heading towards Taiwo. Patting his shoulder, he gave him a hug before turning to Karen and then Tosan, doing the same. Truly, no words were needed. They understood.

Death was a heavy cloak of grief.

Seun sank to the ground near the hospital chair and placed her head on the cool surface, drifting off into a fitful sleep.

She woke up in her own bed and she knew Frank had been there. Uzi slept peacefully in his bed in the corner too. Turning her tear-stained pillow upside down, she proceeded to dampen the other side too with more tears. Frustrated and angry, she threw the pillow off the bed and kicked off her blanket in annoyance. She drifted back into another fitful sleep. With terrible dreams.

***

Apapa, Lagos, Nigeria | February 2020 |

'Do you think she's in heaven?' Seun whispered to Frank, looking at him from behind her shades. They sat in the front row of the small chapel at Temi's Home. It was her funeral service.

'I know she is.' Frank whispered back and squeezed her palm. She squeezed back and nodded, unable to get another word out. Her heart felt heavy and she blinked back tears, dabbing at her swollen eyes. She'd been crying all day.

The preacher's closing words echoed through the small chapel just then as though in agreement with what Frank had said.

'The bible says in 1 Thessalonians 4:14-18 - since we believe that Jesus died and rose, so we also believe that God will bring with him those who have died in Jesus. What we are saying is a message from the Lord: we who are alive and still around at the Lord's coming definitely won't go ahead of those who have died. This is because the Lord himself will come down from heaven with the signal of a shout by the head angel and a blast on God's trumpet. First, those who are dead in Christ will rise. Then, we who are living and still around will be taken up together with them in the clouds to meet with the Lord in the air. That way we will always be with the Lord. So encourage each other with these words.'

All Temi's biological children came up to give their eulogies; Karen, her first daughter from her first marriage- who she'd given up for adoption, had only known for a few years and was the reason she'd set up the home; Anita, her second daughter from her second marriage and Tosan, the last born and only boy, from her second marriage.

Now it was Seun's turn to come up and she couldn't get her legs to move. They felt like spaghetti.

'Hey, you're up.' Frank nudged her.

She nodded and willed herself to get up, walking towards the small podium in slow, calculated steps.

Taking the mic, she started her speech shakily. 'My mother was an amazing woman. She was so strong. And she fought hard for everyone she loved.' She teared up but she kept going. 'She had the biggest smile and I could never understand for the life of me, why she wouldn't get rid of that old rickety thing she called a car.' Pausing, she looked around as everyone laughed through their tears. It had been a famous car.

'I lost count of the number of times I, well, we all...' More laughter. '...told her to change it. But I understand now, what it meant to her. The memories it held with her late husband. It reminds me of how, I want to hold on to everything she ever gave me, hug them and smell her on them. And feel a little closer to her, even though

I know she's gone. And even after they stop smelling like her.' She paused again, to compose herself, dabbing at her eyes carefully.

Frank walked up to her and put his hand on the small of her back for support. 'You're doing great.' He whispered. 'But you look as if you'll fall any moment.'

She turned to him gratefully, but her eyes seemed to say, let-me-do-this. 'I know. But if it's the last thing I ever do for her, then let me do it well.' She whispered back fiercely before once again, facing the congregation.

'Temi was not my biological mother. For many of us here, young and old, she picked us from the messes we were in and gave us new hope for life. She taught us about Jesus and showed us in every way, the true meaning of love. Even though it took some of us so long to accept.' She chuckled slightly as she pointed at herself sheepishly. 'Some of us.' More tears.

'And today, we are not just...sad, for her death. But we are joyful even beyond our pain, and we celebrate the life she lived. Sixty five years may not be a really long time, but Temi lived a thousand lives in one. And I'm happy to call her mother, now and forever.'

Seun let Frank hold her as she broke into tears. The rest of the funeral went by in a blur and she didn't realize when he led her away from the church and to her apartment. They had left the kids with Karen and Taiwo.

As he turned to leave, she held his hand to stop him. 'Don't leave. Please. I don't want to be alone.' Her voice cracked as she said it and she wished she didn't sound so pathetic and needy.

He nodded slowly and followed her inside, locking the door behind him.

'I'm here. I'm not going anywhere.'

Settling her into bed, he lay on a spare mattress on the ground and stared at the ceiling, listening to her breathing slow till he was sure she was fast asleep.

He thought back to his dream and realized what it was. It had been a foreboding. But he'd seen the wrong person. Tears stung his own eyes as he kept replaying it in his head. Temi was gone. For good. And ironically, he felt at peace with the thought. At least she'd lived a full life.

And Seun. Well, she was a whole different ball game. He could tell she was trying and he was grateful for that. But he wasn't at peace.

In that one moment, he knew that he couldn't let her go, not now and not ever again. He loved her with everything in him. And maybe it took a death scare to make him realize how little time there was.

Fireboy's lyrics floated into his head and he pondered on it for a bit.

'Love me while you can, time no dey o, time no dey. It's only once in life. Love me while you can o, time no dey, time no dey o, time no dey…'

Observing her sleeping form, he swept a stray strand of hair from her face and placed a kiss on her forehead.

God help me. Help me to love her.

She murmured in her sleep and reached her hand out, feeling for him, even with her eyes closed. 'Don't leave me.'

He took the hand she held out and placed a kiss there too. 'I won't. Not again.'

Epilogue

The TV interview went way better than she anticipated and the number of TV, radio and podcast invites she got were over the roof. In the end, she could only do a few and she selected them carefully, with Aunty Anna's help. The woman had become more than an editor to her now. She was a friend.

Every now and again as she walked into a mall or restaurant, people stopped her and took selfies.

'Oh my God, it's Tabitha the anon!' The teenage girls were the most enthusiastic bunch but she always indulged them even though she hadn't quite gotten used to the attention. She doubted she ever would.

Of course, there were always the naysayers who looked at her with suspicion, as if to say they didn't believe her 'conversion'. And to be honest, she doubted herself sometimes. But she found strength, in knowing, that perfection was never the goal and she'd never be able to meet up to the world's standards even if she tried.

Jesus' standards though. All she had to do was believe and keep striving to be more like him, daily and with everything she had. Now that; that she could manage.

'So boss, how does it feel to be famous?' Frank teased her.

'Well, it's just there really. I can't quite get used to it.'

'But you've been famous for a long time though.' He pointed out, referring to her viral blog.

'Yeah. Anonymously.' She sighed and looked at him. 'This is different.'

'Well, sounds like fun and money.' Looking at her mischievously, he added, 'Sound familiar?'

'Oh come on Frank.' She laughed and face palmed, remembering their CEO talk months ago. Then she decided to play along. 'But you're right, it is kind of fun and I have to admit, the money is good. But it gets tiring. Sometimes, I just wish I could crawl back into my anonymous shell.'

'Hm.' He simply said, smiling from ear to ear. 'Perks of being your own boss I guess.'

She grinned widely. 'Yeah. But it's not as glamorous as it sounds.'

'Says the bestselling celebrity author,' he pointed at himself, 'to the bloody ex-CEO.' Frank rolled his eyes and she shook her head, laughing quietly.

'Go on, say it. I know you want to.' She nodded and jabbed him playfully. 'Now I know how you felt right?'

'Exactly.'

He parked the car as they got to her parents' house. She hadn't been there in seven years. The place looked old, unkempt and over-run with weeds.

It was an eyesore.

They stood in front of it for long seconds, as silent tears flowed down Seun's cheek. People passed by and stared at them in confusion but neither of them noticed. They were both lost in their own thoughts as they stared at the house, with mixed feelings. The seconds flowed into minutes and still, they stood, hands intertwined.

'It seems so small and insignificant now.' Seun finally said.

'I guess time kind of does that to things. It makes them seem less weighty, it dulls their pain and most importantly, it gives us a chance to focus on the future.'

Yesterday is gone, today is here and tomorrow...well, tomorrow is another day. It might not be the best of days still. But we'll have another chance on tomorrow's tomorrow - the day after tomorrow.

Author's Note

A Love For Tomorrow is set in modern day Nigeria, the largest and arguably most successful African country. This title is unique in the way it came about. I initially planned to call the book 'Tomorrow is Another Day' or 'The Day After Tomorrow' because I am a sucker for metaphors.

But I eventually settled on this title for a variety of reasons - I wanted to state from the onset that this is primarily a love story, I needed 'tomorrow' to be in it (weird I know, but relevant) and I decided to take expert advice on which name worked best. Come to think of it, one of my initial title ideas might have caught your attention more than this did. But I guess we'll never know now. Haha!

Another interesting fact about this book is that I finished writing it in four months. And this is a big deal for me because my first book took me four years to write. And so, this is a move of grace that God used my writing coach, Laju Iren, to aid.

This story is actually Book II in a Christian romance series touching on mental health such as depression, Post Traumatic

Stress Disorder (PTSD) and addiction because it is something that is not given enough attention in this corner of the world. It is a real problem, especially PTSD. Book I is Where the Lotus Grows but they can both be read independent of each other and properly understood.

'70 percent of adults experience at least one traumatic event in their lifetime, 20 percent of people who experience a traumatic event will develop PTSD, about 8 million people have PTSD in a given year and 1 in 13 people will develop PTSD at some point in their life.'

-www.therecoveryvillage.com

Further, the stigma around mental health within many African nations is a huge factor that aids in perpetrating this sad pattern. People are afraid to speak up or seek help for fear of being ostracized by their families and society in general. Many are suffering in silence, self-harming and hurting those around them.

For things to really change, we need to educate ourselves and create an enabling environment for education, diagnosis and treatment.

Thanks for reading.

References
-www.therecoveryvillage.com
-www.google.com

Acknowledgments

To God, the Almighty, for making everything beautiful in His time. To my parents, Elder and Deaconess Ayo and Lara Ogunyinka, for your unending support. To bestselling author and writing coach, Laju Iren, for teaching me well, helping me finish writing this book in record time and reviewing it. I am forever grateful. To Esther Omemu, my best friend, this is an honorable mention, for all you do. To my brother, Hezekiah, for always being in my corner. And to everyone who has ever read any of my work and encouraged me, you are the real MVP. Thank you.

About The Author

Oyinkansola Amazing-Grace Ogunyinka (The Grace Ola) is a dreamer, speaker and avid reader. She has a wild imagination and likes to refer to herself as a hopeless romantic. She has been writing since she was in elementary school and currently provides freelance content writing services to individuals and brands.

She was born in Lagos, Nigeria and spent her high school years in Christ Vision College, Ikorodu, a city located along the Lagos Lagoon in the north-east of the state. She is currently a content developer and brand communications associate at a leading fintech in Nigeria. A graduate of Mass Communication from Covenant University, she majored in Public Relations and Advertising and runs her own content development agency - The Copy Brand. A member of the Covenant University Literary and Debating Society (CULDS), she is one of the contributing authors of the society's 2018 debut anthology 'Black and White' using the pen name 'Grace Ola Oyinkansola'.

Her short story 'You and I' was featured in the August 2017 edition of Writers Space Africa, an online monthly publication. She has also published 'Where the Lotus Grows', the Book 1 of A Love for Tomorrow (the sequel) and has two short stories published on OkadaBooks: 'How the Great Have Fallen' and 'The Room'. She especially loves reading fiction (mostly romance), eating food (ice cream and chocolate is life) and playing.

She wants her books to appeal to people from all walks of life and her goal is to write the Father's heart (God), one word at a time.

□

Meet Oyinkansola A. Ogunyinka (The Grace Ola)

Visit thegraceola.com to read her over 100 short stories, articles and reviews. Learn more about Oyinkansola and stay connected by following her via:

Instagram: @thegraceola

Twitter: @thegraceola

LinkedIn: Oyinkansola A. Ogunyinka

Facebook: Oyinkansola A. Ogunyinka (The Grace Ola)

OkadaBooks: Oyinkansola A. Ogunyinka

www.thegraceola.com